Tales of
Indifference

Tales of
Indifference

An Anthology of SULTRY, SECRETIVE, & SIMPLISTIC Short Stories

· · · · · · · · · · · · · · · · · · ·

Tracey 'Girlz'

authorHOUSE®

AuthorHouse™ LLC
1663 Liberty Drive
Bloomington, IN 47403
www.authorhouse.com
Phone: 1-800-839-8640

Published by AuthorHouse   09/11/2013

ISBN: 978-1-4918-1513-7 (sc)
ISBN: 978-1-4918-1512-0 (hc)
ISBN: 978-1-4918-1511-3 (e)

Library of Congress Control Number: 2013916374

FROM THE AUTHOR

Who is to say that when we begin any venture it will turn out as we anticipate? Who is to say dreams can't actually come to fruition? Do we have to truly have supporters in our corner to believe it's a corner of reality?

Over my life, I have always known that <u>one thing</u> I must do while on this quest for 'life' was to write a book. As I have ventured into unveiling such an endeavor, I know it was God's unique path of my interesting life that has led me to accepting and pressing positively in such a special direction.

To answer the posed questions; (1) only faith is what leads us to begin the venture for those things that seem impossible are a mere mustard seed away, (2) only we are to say dreams can't come to fruition because without action nothing is possible, and (3) it's sometimes those negative forces that build us to having unparallel strength; for not all will be cheerful and rave but along the journey they will see the reality.

Tracey 'Girlz'

<u>First, are the following acknowledgments . . .</u>

To Dominique (my gem) & Angel (my angelic one),

The two of you are my precious, beautiful, and intelligent daughters. You are so different yet your similarities are quite apparent despite the significant age difference. I earnestly pray that you (both) sincerely know that your rough edges will yet turn smooth if you yet believe. May you never quit, never give up, nor accept failure for the Master holds you firmly and I have been blessed to have you, hold you, and honor you with His omnipotent being. I challenge you both to always dream big for destiny begins with that dream; equally so, striving and never accepting defeat is the solution to any given dilemma. I love you both today and always . . .

To Sandra,

My *second mom, sister, and true lifelong friend* . . . your support has been the catalyst to my drive. Your unwavering love has aided in my solid foundation. Your consistency has been second to none. For these things, I eternally say 'thank you'.

To Mary,

My *Pan-Hellenic sister and my true friend* . . . your editorial critique and consults have been priceless. Your words of finite wisdom in terms of word selection have been a driving force to enable this to become a reality. Your stand for me when others said 'no' will yet never go forgotten. For these things, I eternally say 'thank you'.

To Sirena,

My *God-sister but closer than blood* . . . your words to remind me that you admire me for forging in courage and excelling above what others would ever see in me has stuck in my mind heavily. From the moment you heard the sincerity in my voice about this project, you cheered me on. From the second I said I needed your assistance, you never hesitated. From the moment I would waiver, you would shower me with protective words and sent powerful prayer my way. For these things, I eternally say 'thank you'.

To Angela,

My *blood cousin but a sister in deed* . . . you have always been my inspiration for teaching and demonstrating it's essential to be true to oneself and never giving up. In the midst of it all, your encouragement and support has caused me to realize that we should sometimes step away to step right. For those things, I eternally say 'thank you'.

To my *dear and special friend* along with so many others . . . For some of you, you say much. For one in particular, you do so much and say so little, *yet it all is so great*. I couldn't have gotten this far without any of my special connections who will forever be close to my heart. For that, I eternally say 'thank you'.

Then, I, as the author, feel compelled to share this thought . . .

From birth to conception; this work has been a labor of love. Each original and quite unique story tells a story and has its own purpose. ***He who has little or a lot is not moved to wither as the plant of growth can survive and thrive with the proper nourishment*** . . .

MY DEDICATION—**THE FATHER** . . .

For I know without Him, this would not have been possible. As early as I could fathom logical thoughts and ideas, I knew that my thirst was great and I hungered for more. I have always desired to strive hard in any and everything I have done. But to accept less than that continuously left me empty. Truly, in any action or deed, I knew he had placed a greater calling on me. The culmination of difficulties, trials, smiles, and life have not been in vain. When I yet felt alone, He would blow a bit of courage my way. When I yet felt like giving up, He would give me something else to try. When I felt like I was confused, He said he was shaking me up for greatness. For, _the prayers and sleepless nights did not go in vain . . . this anthology of short stories (book) is just the beginning . . ._

Contents

Chapter I

Best Friends

Darrell, Horton, and Clifton had been inseparable since 3rd grade. If you saw one, the other two were near. They joined the same teams in school; dodge ball, chess club, and intramural activities. They called each other's family their own as this was just second nature. They even typically dated sisters to prevent having to drive too far. Once Horton had dated someone and her ex-beau came by and stirred up trouble for Darrell. He forwarded his friends a quick message via his phone and they immediately showed up. They had one another's' back. So, cynicism regarding the particular of the location of dates may be the perception of some. But in their minds, they preferred to be near one another due to the protection and closeness they held for one another. That type of brotherly love was simply unheard of.

If a fight ensued, all would fight. If an argument arose outside their sect, all would comment. If the teachers expelled one, the other two would do something unimaginable to also gain expulsion. Once Clifton intentionally lied about having drugs on his person *(he truthfully found a marijuana cigarette in the boys' bathroom and picked it up)* in an attempt to get into trouble. This was because he was determined to be near his friend, Darrell, who was definitely in trouble as he had supposedly brought a weapon to school to protect himself from classroom bullies. This one day in particular Darrell refused to take being pushed, having his money taken, and being tortured by the neighborhood gang. Even more importantly, he was adamant that Clifton and Horton wouldn't get into trouble for his retalitative spirit. This was far beyond his control. Horton had already devised a plan to get in trouble for the day. He had intentionally copied off the smartest girl in the class' test which he knew the teacher would be furious about and definitely would send him immediately to detention or have him sent home for a day or so.

Lest we pretend they never disagreed, they had their battles. However, the unaffected person would always force the two to make up. Once Darrell told Horton that Clifton had fallen, broken his ankle, and was flown to the neighboring town due to the severity of an accident. Of course, Horton was on high alert and very anxious. Despite being upset with Clifton, Horton couldn't bare his friend being hurt. Lest known, he not be there, regardless of being frustrated with him or not. When he arrived at Mrs. Tureen' home, she was shocked to see Horton at her door in such a sheer frantic state. "Calm down sweetie, he is going to be okay", she told him. Horton couldn't understand her calmness since he thought Clifton had been flown away due to some alleged horrific accident. In a matter of minutes, he saw Clifton on the big mauve suede couch propped up on the beige and brown pillows. He ran to him and apologized for their misunderstanding. He had forgotten he was misled by their other friend. All Horton knew was he didn't like the thought of his best friend being ill. They did their bosom buddy friend handshake and mutually expressed regrets for their behaviors.

Growing up in their rural community was quite special. Back in the day, they frequented each others homes so of course the families were very close. The same love that was shown for one was distributed equally amongst them all. Likewise, if one got in trouble in the neighborhood, the matriarch of each family, would 'tighten' the guilty party up until he got home. Of course, the offender received it again at that time as well.

The relationship of the three was probably predestined even prior to their existence for their mothers had gone to middle and high school together in that small town. They were cheerleaders together, joined the same clubs, and typically dated best friends. Coincidentally, when Mrs. Roberson (formerly Ms. Patrick/her maiden name), Horton's mother married and became pregnant with Horton almost 4 months later to the date Darrell's mother had conceived him as well. Soon after that, Clifton's mother followed suit.

Horton was the oldest. He was recently offered multiple scholarships because of his football prowess. His most recent love was Tammy. She was the first female he dated who didn't fall into the 'sisters' cache. At 21, he felt truly at peace. His family was excited as his collegiate choice, FSU, as this was his mothers' Alma Mata.

Clifton was the shortest of the three. He stood only 5'5 ½" tall but yet stood tall in his group. As he would speak, his hazel eyes, pearly white teeth, brown low-hair cut, and perfect smile lit up any room despite his miniature statuesque. His voice radiated power and that's why he was forsaking his wrestling scholarship to focus on a career in law. Family law was his dream. At 20, his collegiate choice was Alabama A&M.

Oddly enough, off the court, Darrell was the shyest of the triad. Well, that was only true if he was alone. With his two buddies, he would boast, cheer, yell, and rave like any other 21 year old full-blooded healthy male. At 6'3", Darrell was the epitome of power on the court. He averaged 35 points a game, 12 assists, 10 rebounds, held a 80% FT average, and an astonishing 90% 3-point average with typically 5-7 powerful '3s' at his discretion against any opponent.

Darrell had toughness on the court, shyness off the court, but a true marshmallow when he saw someone he truly liked. She was about 5'8" tall, a beautiful Halle Berry hair cut, and eyes like Jennifer Lopez. She was a foreign student whom he had laid eyes on during freshman experience weekend upon visiting Florida A&M. Sadly enough, she hadn't yet connected the dots back to him but his hopes were beaming with internal excitement. That weekend was magical and his infatuation was immense for a girl whom he only knew her name, Tammy. But it sounded oh so melodic in his mind. She now became the greatest reason, other than basketball, to return to school officially this fall.

This last summer togetherness meant the world to the three of them. It was the end of the beginning, and beginning of the end. For this month, these best friends would have to begin finding themselves and place a tight seal on some of their escapades as they were near there adventurous end. Soon, late nights would no longer exist, no more dating in symmetry, and even the overprotective nature would have to calm down. On the positive side, they were still going to be relatively close in proximity as the schools they selected were in Florida and Alabama. This was intentional as time wise they could yet visit one another in less than 4 hours each.

"Clifton, get the door man. Do you not hear that annoying doorbell?" yelled Darrell from upstairs. Surprisingly, they were all home on this Saturday morning. They truly enjoyed the comfort of their 2-story loft that they rented the last semester of the senior year in high school. All of their parents agreed since they couldn't seem to be separated anyway. This loft wasn't the usual bachelor pad some may think. It was neat and tidy simply because they all grew up with that being a priority from their grandmothers' who lived in each home. It was very spacious; 3 full baths, 3 average-sized bedrooms, ceiling fans in each bedroom, and open bay windows. To be honest, it did have one atypical feature of most young men; a partially empty refrigerator. This was at least until one of the mothers' would come over, visiting and then restock it accordingly. Outsiders would assume they don't work, but all three of them work and enjoy it wholeheartedly.

It chimed again. The doorbell rang a third and fourth time. At the door stood a naval military officer, with a stern yet consoling look on his face. Within moments, the friends' lives would change forever as they once knew it.

"Sir, I'm looking for Mr. Horton Randall", the gentleman stated. "Uh, uh, uh", Clifton stuttered. He shook his head and tried to quickly regain his composure. "Would you like to come in?" Clifton asked the officer as he was still standing outside the door. He walked with such form and flawless posture; shoes shined to perfection and dress blues as neat as any suit just picked up from the cleaners but still on the white paper hanger.

Within moments, Horton and Darrell came in simultaneously. The two of them just stopped and looked at one another. All Clifton could do was stand as he knew Horton had a brother and sister in the navy. He also had two other relatives in the Air Force but his father had died in a war when he was only 2 years old. Horton had no idea that this gentleman who stood holding his top hat in hand was there for him. Though, Darrell was in shock as well because his father was serving a high ranking naval position in Germany. To date, he had already served over 20 years.

The only sound in the room was the clock that sat on a nearby end table. It was small in size but at that moment the *'tick, tock'* was ever so loud. With hearts beating, palms sweating, and knots in their stomach, the 45 seconds of silence seemed like an eternity.

"Mr. Randall, Mr. Horton Randall", he continued. He looked at both Darrell and Horton because he wasn't sure who to address. Then, within a flash, Horton just buckled to the floor. He couldn't take it. He was having intense palpitations which seemed like a heart attack, the frog in his throat seemed like he had swallowed an apple, and the knot in his stomach and pain in his heart were too powerful.

Clifton and Darrell stood motionless listening to the officer detailing the death of his 25 year old sister who was killed by friendly fire. Brandi had already served 6 years and was on a mission in Uganda. The only words that resonated from his voice were " . . . *Officer Brandi Horton was a remarkable soldier and will be missed and loved by all . . .*" All they could think was this was supposed to be her last overseas mission for at least 2 years. All three had planned to go see her when she returned to the states. Her nickname was "Brae" by all who loved her.

Horton eventually got up off the floor. He moved ever so slowly to the green oversized chair. He picked up his family photo and stared at it. He looked at his buddies and said, "Is it true? Did that officer actually come here and say my baby sister, Brae, is gone? She is my baby sister. I love her and . . ." his voice just crackled.

Off in the distance, Darrell could hear Horton's cell phone ring. He was sure it was his mother calling to comfort him. "Hello, Ma Randall", Darrell said without hesitation. "Uh, what, what did you say ma'am? This is who?" he muttered. Clifton glided over to him as he was sliding because he had only had on his clean, white basketball socks which regularly would cause him to glide along the shiny linoleum floor. Coincidentally, this entire week, they had taken the time to clean the home from top to bottom. They had just scheduled a camping trip to wrap up personal loose ends with one another and begin to make corresponding emotional strides into adulthood.

The phone call was another shocker. The female had just told Darrell that Ms. Hampton had suffered a heart attack last night. Unfortunately, this was just days after learning her cancer had progressed. The caller, who was Horton's aunt, yet asked Clifton who had taken the phone from Darrell about Horton's behavior and informed him that his mother had been crying for him in her sleep.

The next morning, Horton's clock beeped and beeped. From the nearby distance, you could hear Darrell and Clifton both yelling for him to shut it off. It had been 15-20 minutes of continuous ringing.

Darrell got to his door first. "Hey Ton", he called through the door. "Could you please hit that clock before I hit you with it"? There was no response. Clifton walked up, wearing his high school basketball shorts, rubbing his eyes, and trying to snap himself into a fully awake state. He turned to Darrell and asked him if he had heard that sound last night. Darrell responded with "Man, you know it was probably the neighbors. They are always partying during the week. Luckily, we wait till the weekend to have our sets".

Clifton opened the door and saw him. He was stunned, shocked, and startled. He was gone. Darrell yelled "No". That scream was louder than the sound of most 2-year old toddlers running from a parent insisting on feeding them beets.

Horton was stretched across his bed with his 9mm laid on the floor. The bullet wound was too surreal. Motionless, rigid, and still; he was gone. The note read:

I am sorry all. Clifton and Darrell I will love you forever. Tell Mom and Kenny, Jr. that I do love them and will miss them as well. Guys, it was hard enough to temporarily lose the two of you but today was just too much. This was supposed to be the beginning of the end and the end of the beginning. But in a good way, so what happened? My mother has less than a year left with her cancer. I had been seeing this in dreams but I thought it was all in my head. Her heart attack is going to leave her too weak to even fight that disease. Kenny is still in jail and doesn't understand the ramifications of his actions on the family. Now, today, Brandi's death . . . I just can't be a true part of the triad anymore. My strength is gone. My fight for life is gone. My power is gone. But guys, my love will eternally be with the two of you but truly my heart has shattered beyond repair.

After the death of their best friend, Clifton and Darrell experienced some dramatic changes in their lives as well. Darrell's mother went through a tremendous depression. Coupled with her depression, Mrs. Barker lost her husband to a hit and run accident as he was simply walking back to the car in the parking lot from her office building. The driver was never caught so closure for her seemed impossible. When Horton passed, it was the final straw for her. She deemed inpatient treatment for some time. Clifton's mother was yet trying to be the backbone from their threesome. She spent as much time as possible with her two girlfriends, Claire (Randall) and Patrice (Barker).

With everything going on in their lives, Clifton and Darrell both changed their minds regarding college. With their mothers going through so much mentally and physically, they felt simply compelled to be able to do something to benefit their lives on a more permanent basis. At the minimum, they wanted to understand the psyche from which these concerns were based from a medical and clinical perspective.

By the spring, they had both discussed their recent occurrences and merged back into the oneness they had held for so many years. Clifton and Darrell reapplied and were both accepted at University of Tennessee. Clifton chose to major in psychology and Darrell now medicine. They made a commitment to each other that they had to do as much as possible to help their families moving forward and to not let their friend, Horton's death be in vain. *Why didn't he share his feelings? Why had he chosen to end his life?* Those questions may never get the answers they both deemed. As a result, they swore to never separate; marriage or death was the only way. Interestingly enough, the triad had attained one new member, Tammy. With Horton's death, she needed a friend. The most obvious choice was his two best friends. They embraced her sisterly and tried their best to become the brothers she never had.

Chapter II

Just In Time

Mr. Smythe was so funny when it came to his animals. He regularly named the female animals' names similar to his former schoolmates. This was his reconnection to the past. Most of his current adults' friends thought it was weird.

Amanda was his newest delivery. She was a 5 pound baby ewe. An ewe is most commonly known as a lamb or female sheep. She was white in color and had the biggest, prettiest round eyes. As a result, this newest addition to his farm—Amanda was named for his second grade crush. He never forgot her. She had the most noticeable eyes and gentle tone.

Life on the farm wasn't new for him as he had inherited it from Uncle Bobby. He had grown up visiting his favorite uncle every summer out there and he felt right at home. Uncle Bobby was failing in health and had decided Carl should take it over now while he still lived. In his will, it had already been established to be enforced with the same permanency.

Carl lived with his girlfriend, Mary, out there and she was a true country girl. She enjoyed the space and freedom to be free of inner city traffic, close neighbors, and noisy relatives. Carl's son, Robert, was away in college and doing quite well. He was a third year engineer student at Michigan State. Mary had no biological children but had adopted one son at the age of 20. He was away on an extended internship through his college, Penn State.

"Tomorrow, we are going in the city for a night out Mary", said Carl. Carl longed for some romance as the relationship had felt stagnated. They fed the animals, cleaned the stalls, and washed them all accordingly. This was in addition to picking the eggs from the chicks and occasionally falling in the mud while caring for the pigs. But the oneness and connection most 40ish year old couples should be experiencing was missing.

Mary loved him. But was empty inside and at this point she didn't care nor understand the reason. In her mind, she was just comfortable and existing. She couldn't work a regular 9-5 because of her speech difficulties and bipolar issues. Her moods fluctuated as often as days of the week. She doesn't regularly see a physician which adds to the barriers which exist for her.

Robert was loving school. With this being his 3rd year, he was now more acclimated to collegiate life. He wasn't athletically inclined but truly academically intellectual. He received a Presidential award for excellence his first year at Michigan State. At the beginning of this semester, his grade point average (GPA) was 4.3. This was simply phenomenal for most in majors as intense as engineering.

He recently experienced something quite wonderful that he had yet to share with his father whom he rarely kept secrets. He had become serious with a pre-med student, Joyce, and was finding himself growing into his own. He recently moved off campus and enjoyed that independence. He was reluctant to tell his father because he knew he was yet overprotective and would assume he would become distracted with drugs or sex if not grounded on campus.

Jason was Mary's adopted son and she held the same pride for him that any natural parent does for their child. He was a remarkable child. He, too, was extremely smart. He skipped several grades in school and entered college early. Jason had become a father at the age of 16, but he was already in college and on the way to providing for him. He currently works 2 part-time jobs and goes to school full-time. Prior to the birth of his son, he had managed to stay away from trouble or upsetting his mother due to foolishness. Although all was surprised at the announcement of this little one, he has yet been treated as a pure blessing.

Mary decided to call her sister and inquire about pre-menopause. She told her she had been having irregular cycles and more unusual emotional changes. With the cuts in Medicaid, she was reluctant to go and see her physician although having more and more irregularities but realizing they wouldn't heal themselves.

The farm animals all seemed to have their own schedule. At 4 a.m., it wasn't just the hens and chickens ready for the new day. But this particular Thursday, was a little odd. It came in sets of two and timing was the key. The pregnant rabbits, cows, and horses all went into labor simultaneously. What on earth were they to do?

Carl was just cool. He never lost his composure. He got his schedule prepped and checked each one accordingly. The cows were first and he got ready. Probably not 10 minutes later, he could hear the horses. Sandy his favorite horse was brown and black. She was a beautiful Appaloosa and only 7 years old. Within moments, Jason and Robert walked in. They had both decided to surprise their parents even though they communicated with one another about this trip. It was an extended weekend as it was the Easter break for them both. They jumped in hands first. By the end of this wonderful 3 hour experience, 7 new animals were bore. Six females and 1 male became a part of the Smythe family.

It went without saying; Carl would keep with his tradition. He went to his handy book to see what names he had already used and to see where he stood in terms of naming these. According to Carl, he was into his junior high female friends but he had oddly forgotten a couple of elementary buddies. So, the chosen names were Carmella, Darla, Heather, Brandy, Sarah, and Tiffany. The male name had no rhyme or reason so it was just Bo.

Dinner was normally scheduled for 5 p.m. but tonight they were all going into the city and eat as a family. The two collegiate males had always gotten along great. Their parents had been together for about 6 years now and had watched them grow for quite some time.

At home this trip, Jason had definite plans to spend most of his time with Ja'son, his only child. He was almost 6 now and growing up almost overnight. His mother ensured he regularly spoke with his father and helped him realize that Jason hadn't abandoned him despite being away at school. This was as extremely important to Jason as he never had a father in his life. But without this education, he couldn't provide the type of life Ja'son deserved.

After dinner, Mary decided to make a confession to the three men in her life. She told them she was back on her Seroquel for her depression, was going to begin taking Ambien for her sleeplessness, and had scheduled an appointment another physician for her communication difficulties. She said, "My general doctor doesn't know what is going on with my communication. He said it could be neurological as it has changed over time. But he ran blood work and is going to call me with another referral on next week". They all look at her with pride and each took turns kissing her affectionately on the cheek.

Robert decided to also open up and reveal his secret. He announced he was in love. He told them her name is Joyce and he planned to propose next Valentine's Day. He explained how they truly have a bond and their relationship is vested strong by a solid friendship.

Carl was surprisingly calm. He looked up and said, "I am happy for you, son". They embraced and hugged like it was the first day he had left for school.

By next weekend, Mary had gone to see her grandson. She enjoyed the time she spent with Ja'son. He was a typical little boy who enjoyed football and eating hamburgers. He had a low hair cut and was neatly dressed in appearance. They did everything from going to the movies to visiting Chucky Cheese.

That Christmas, both boys came home and even Ja'son was there for the celebration. Robert's girlfriend, Joyce, even came home this year. She was embraced by all and within moments she felt right at home. The 6' tree was fully decorated and had plenty of gifts underneath. The yard was filled with festive decorations and colorful lights around the home.

By evening, after dinner, Carl and Mary surprised the boys this time with their own announcement. They had planned to get married on New Year's Eve.

Chapter III

The Twins Said It Best

The prior (4) individuals had each walked up and gave remarks as friends, neighbors, colleagues, and family. As Sgt. Biscoe stood at the podium, he paused momentarily and all in attendance could see the two streaks of tears glistening on his cheeks. This was a little odd considering this 6'4", 205 lb. chiseled athletic 15 year veteran of the Air Force seemed so well put together. His prior 2 minute speech had been about the experiences from college with his wonderful literature professor. But it took a wonderful turn when he revealed that this person also helped him search for his half-brother, encouraged him to write a poetry book, and mentored him as he developed a special program for lost teens upon his retiring from the military almost 5 years ago now.

As he was about to walk away, he jokingly shared comical moments the two men shared via phone and Skype on occasion. He emphasized they profoundly held a certain level of professional spirit and comfort for one another. But to his chagrin, he admitted he had known this loss would take something away from his being because he had always been the father he longed for. He warily told the audience that their rapport and connection was such that he could not have fathomed the prodigious and ostentatious Professor Lawrence Greenwood to leave this earth prior to his personal demise.

The sound within the room had changed from a chuckle, to snicker, to laugh, to sniffles all within a matter of seconds.

Oddly enough, the next sound and visual was of two identical twins walking in unison and hand in hand. They pulled out what appeared to be a journal and placed it upon the black and white stand. To some, black and white may appear to be an odd color for the décor of the day. But the late Professor's daughter, who was a designer, knew he only spoke and thought either in black or white because he always chose to give individuals the benefit of the doubt. He revered and admired colors for what they were and the beauty them implored as an expression of the splendor of life. They appeared to be about 17 years old but their smooth skin may have caused a little deceit for one to speculate at their age without having a bit of fact. Obviously, this well-known man had left an impact on individuals of all ages. This particular ceremony was reminiscent of that fact.

The brother and sister duo wore matching black and white tuxedo suits but beheld a colorful small boutonniere of colored roses in their coordinating pockets. They didn't look like they were going to a wedding or another stuffy affair. But they looked crisp and classy and would have made him proud. They turned to one another and said, "We can do this". The audience knew at that moment they were in for a treat. In succession, they turned towards the large picture of their mentor, placed a yellow rose upon the silver box which beheld flowers from memories of his acquaintances from the prior ceremony, and lovingly blew a kiss towards the late Professor Greenwood and his daughter whom they had come to affectionately know quite well.

The program identified the two as Darrell and Destinee, two of Professor Greenwood's favorite mentees. In harmony, they both stated, "Ladies and Gentlemen, we recognize memorial services are not traditionally conducted in this manner. But he wasn't an atypical individual. So, could you each please transcend into this personal journey with us? We need you to close your eyes, allow yourselves to feel, see, and smell these words as they were written flawlessly by someone clearly loved and respected by us all."

> ***Beauty in its purest form*** . . . *The bible speaks in symbolism of a woman's hair being her glory. The fortunate thing is that due to the uniqueness of a woman, each person has yet to define the creativity of who she is and how she wants to be viewed. Some choose to keep short locks. Some choose to keep medium layers. Some choose to have long tresses. With varying textures, does hair really define who a woman is? If an individual loses their hair due to an illness such as cancer or*

*a medication side effect, is she any less significant? If an individual is asked to wear a wig because of a performance either in college or Broadway, have they lessened their ability to express their creativity? Hair is simply fine, thin like strands which begin in the epidermis of our skin. The bible has many versus which elaborate about cutting or covering of the head. It also denotes discussions of interest relating to women adorning themselves. I will not proclaim to be the bearer to express how women should see themselves. But I will always suggest that if beauty is within the eye of the beholder then that should begin the discussion of glorifying oneself. Hair or not; beauty is an anecdotal element which is deep within. As I said, **beauty in its purest form!!!***

Beauty in its purest form *. . . At the moment a mother finds out she is with child, a multiplicity of thoughts and acts occur. A father too undergoes this metamorphosis. Lest I acknowledge, the in-depth challenges and perils of this embryo seeking to take form as a little one within marked time.*

As I envision a baby who seeks to finalize the birthing process, he/she becomes less dependent upon mother for its existence. The need for nurturing, protection, and reassurance has an entirely different role. Thoughts and fantasies as well as hopes and dreams; conversely, fears and apprehensions run amuck. Joy takes fold when a mom looks down at her miracle for the first time. Fathers and other family members initially look helplessly at the little one who is actually the helpless one. Delight for all becomes inevitable as soon as a baby can open his or her eyes. That little being looks up and smiles at the simplicity and security of their parent gazing down at them in amazement. It is medically spoken that a newborn can only see black and white for a while. However, over time, the pupils slowly begin to formulate colors. Yet, from the moment a baby leaves the wound, every individual around them begins the process of slow touches and soft whispers. This allows them to immediately ascertain the gentleness that lies within the new world they have encountered.

They have a special cry for food, comfort, sleep, and nurturing; what an amazing ability. The response to the baby who is undoubtedly in need of appropriate engagement is either learned or innate. This isn't to say an individual who has already had a child will or will not respond the same way. This isn't to say an individual who didn't natural bore the child can't love the child the same. For truly, any parent immediately glances in pride at the thought of the possibilities and forecast of the future ahead with their baby. The softness of the baby is like none other. Very often, that purity and impeccable touch is compared to cotton balls or billowy clouds. So often the smell of a baby is something adults yearn to indulge in at every phase of their development. Baby powder and baby lotion are kept within the home long after that initial time when their smell is accentuated by these gentle scents. The beauty of a baby is second to none. As I said, **beauty in its purest form!!!**

Beauty in its purest form *. . . Why is it that leaves present with such odd shapes? They crackle, break, bend, and sometimes dissipate when we smash them within our hands but they somehow always revive themselves onto the same branches the following season. Some are green, yellow, brown, red, and even gold. You can see them as you travel throughout the city, drive across the country, walk through the backyard, glance up into the trees, look in seasonal books, and even notice the attractiveness of certain fields and pastures which all relay the same prettiness during the Summer/Fall transition. That being, the leaves which beautify our trees will inevitably fall and die out but for a season. But they are actually there for many reasons and we should all enjoy their style and shape for no (2) are identical; similar to individuals. So, let's revel in perfection yet imperfection which is amongst us all. Who will get the rake next? Who will jump in the leaf pile next? Who will actually look at the vast colors which exist amongst corresponding trees and limbs? As I said,* **beauty in its purest form!!!**

Beauty in its purest form . . . *One of the purest perfections ever created by the Creator was that of the butterfly. Many children sit down and gawk at a wiggly species that they are only able to fathom as being a caterpillar. Upon picking it up, it becomes apparent that it is harmless. It poses no harm to the body, the skin, or the psyche. It yet draws upon the creative mind to wonder how it goes from mere centimeters to having impeccable phenomenal wings of unique color combinations. Caterpillars communicate with ants. This was something most don't realize in the understanding of this insect. While still caterpillars, they spend most of their time in search of food. But as the transformation begins to take place, butterflies begin to have their own needs. Although they heavily depend upon plant leaves for food, their shape and identification is remarkable all on its own. Unlike other insects, they don't cause unpleasant scents or harmful diseases upon human contact, but instead they express themselves as exemplifying the loveliness of God's creations. How do we as individuals transform ourselves? When do we allow such to take place? Regardless of our answers, it's nice to go back into our youth and appreciate the innocence of this creation in its most basic form. As I said,* **beauty in its purest form!!!**

Beauty in its purest form . . . *How does one describe the blueness seen in the ocean and lakes? Scientifically speaking, the surface of the water reflects the color of the sky. Yet this isn't the only reason it appears blue. It has been proven some constituents of sea water can influence the shade of blue of the ocean. This is why the shade of blue, even viewed as green, varies in different areas. To some, we express this hue as either turquoise, aqua, light, or even ultraviolent. Irrespective of the choice of explanation of the shade; it's most accurately communicated by most as being magnificence in its finest state. Oceans and lakes allude to openness like nothing else. Its color is just a slight expression of its vast possibility. Depth within its base or to ponder an experience atop its nature we can all agree that it has a beauty that is simply flawless at its greatest core. As I said,* **beauty in its purest form!!!**

Darrell and Destinee stopped and looked up at the audience. They asked everyone to open their eyes. Then they both read harmoniously a personal passage. "We love and respect our friend and mentor, Professor Lawrence Greenwood. We acknowledge we are not speaking in past tense. (Everyone giggled as they admitted they were speaking as if he were still present). This is because he will always live with us. Many people told us we were ugly and would never be anything. Many people belittled us for having menial grades prior to us becoming co-valedictorians of our graduating classes. Many people told us we had weird toes, big ears, and odd shaped eyes. But he helped us see the beauty in which we are. For it took time to admit it to ourselves but we couldn't go back in and recreate how we looked. [The 'AMEN FROM THE AUDIENCE' was imminent and louder as they spoke.] We marveled at his works. We marveled at his ability to touch others both in the classroom and out. Most of all we are proud of sharing, in part, a few excerpts from an upcoming book he has recently self-published entitled "Beauty Lies within Our Walls". He impacted our lives, caused us each to accomplish goals that many would deem too difficult, challenged the plausible and caused us to ponder the meaningless and various facets of life which are definitely too great to overlook despite our tender age of 28 years old. (They looked at each other and smiled.)"

At that very moment, Professor Greenwood's daughter knew the phrase **"HE ALWAYS WROTE ABOUT BEAUTY"** would have to be the epitaph to be placed on his permanent resting place irrespective of him being cremated. The entire mood was now peaceful and calm as was her dad. It wasn't about the music or eulogy but the permanent words that he had placed in his journal which would be placed in estate, in partial, along with his being.

Chapter IV

The Blood

As dawn was nearing, Chris was awakened to an odd stench. With his eyes not quite alert; he could feel a slight twinge in his back and ache in his legs. With this being mid March, it wasn't surprising for there to be a slight chill in the room for just three weeks ago, Dallas of all places, had just endured its second unusual snow dusting of the year.

Upon doing his morning stretch routine, he realized that something was wrong. He couldn't feel the headboard. He always performed the same exercises while in the bed as advised by one of his favorite TV shows, Dr. Wonder. That exercise explicitly detailed how everyone should slowly stretch before fully arising each and every morning in order to alleviate further aches and pains throughout the day.

Chris slowly rubbed his eyes and neck and at that moment he actually saw the problem. He was upright in his chair. Although the large brown leather recliner in his bedroom was plush, it wasn't his California king size bed that he normally sprawled perpendicular against after the apple of his eye left for work.

"What's going on?" he muttered. In his head he was truly caught off guard. He truly couldn't remember how he gotten from his bed to his chair. At that time, he noticed his hands were sticky and felt sweaty. Upon looking down, he saw his clothes were different. He had on a gray Chaps shirt and maroon sweats. This was so unlike his norm.

What happened to his usual black silk pajama bottoms that he normally slept in? Where was his black tee that matched so perfectly to those enticing pants? In the bare, his body was totally rippled and toned. He had a flawless 6-pack that caused the guys in the gym to even take a second glance. His legs had minimal hair and muscular in tone; thighs were strong and tight; and biceps and triceps would make any woman want to swoon and deem a little fainting routine to incite his strength to overtake her weakness. Nightly, he would oil up his muscle machine with gentle body dew that he had gotten from a friend who sold Passion Parties after taking his nightly scolding hot shower. But that particular Wednesday night something was off. But he was unsure what and why?

Chris was normally so meticulous in appearance. Shirts always neatly starched with a crisp collar. Slacks always had a matching belt and color coordinated socks. Even his nightwear was perfect. He had several silk pajamas as well as boxers with color coordinating tanks. That was just his style. He prided himself on impeccable grooming. That was one of the few memories he had of his father. His dad reminded him repeatedly to always take pride in your appearance. Occasionally, he would stand in the mirror and almost hear his voice in his head echoing either an approval or disapproval of his clean shaven face and neat goatee that regularly caused even his bros to make comment. Despite the fact that his father died when he was only 8, he had such fond memories. This was just the type of man he was as he even took pride in being neat to go workout. So, how did he end up with his workout pants on this morning?

He stood up and immediately saw it. It was blood. There was dried blood on his hands. The shirt was partially tattered and his favorite maroon sweats, which were a mainstay for his workout wardrobe, had a cut in the left leg almost 2" in diameter. This look was definitely off.

Chris was one of these men who felt proud that he had arisen from a moderate background. He purposefully selects the proper music, friends, associates, and activities. He wouldn't be caught dead using profane language publicly. He wouldn't be caught dead drinking beer publicly. Smoking and drugs were definitely not a part of his persona. He just wouldn't be caught dead doing things that would normally have a stigma associated with them. It's not that he considers himself better than the rest, but because his clients spend up to $500,000 on his services daily, his reputation is imperative to maintain.

Across the room the phone rang and he was ever so startled. First, he had apparently slept in his chair and this was quite unusual. Next, he found himself in clothing he couldn't explain. And now, of all things the phone was ringing. Who on earth could be calling this time of morning?

"Mr. Thompson, are you okay? You are late for your 8:00 appointment with your new client." Clearing his voice, he responded, "Lila, I must have overslept. I'll be in shortly. What time is it?" The female voice stressed, "Its 9 a.m. sir. Do you want me to keep them here?" Stuttering a bit, slumped over now, and rubbing his perfect black hair he stated, "Yes, yes, please. Could you please offer pastries, juice, and distribute a copy of the agenda? Please express my apologies and inform them I was held up in morning traffic." She giggled. Within moments, they hung up the phone.

That drive into work was odd. Thoughts were racing and agony was the culprit of the morning. But getting ready for demonstrating his record of being elite, perfect, and on-point was on the agenda for sure. His ability to project sheer subtly was his mantra so he couldn't let on to his clients that his morning had gone awry.

After the meeting, he came out of the room smiling and glistening with joy. It happened again staff. He looked at his efficient and very talented Administrative Assistant, Lila and partner, Johnny Glimmer and expressed to them that he had just procured another winning contract. This time for $1.2 million in concierge services with that client and his accompanying staff from Mexico. The services are varied and it may even mean expansion of the firm.

"Lila, please order lunch today on me" he said pompously. It's your proficiency in part that has flourished this organization. He looked up with pride at the plate on the wall—THOMPSON & ASSOCIATES; *Concierge Extraordinaire . . .*

Chris and his staff enjoyed lunch and had elected to unwind some. No formalities and no structure. It was finally time to relax a bit.

Within moments, she could see her best girl approaching from across the way. She motioned for her to move in her direction. "Hey sweetie, how are you? I am so glad you agreed to have lunch with me", Shasta said with a smile. After blowing and removing her black, Dolce & Gabana sunglasses, Kathy smiled back and gave her a girlie smooch on each cheek. Shasta was glowing today. Her hair was blowing in the wind ever so elegantly. She was a little more particular about her eyewear. So, instead of removing her Roberto Cavalli Snake sunglasses and placing them on the table, Shasta chose to put them back in their case as to put them on her head may stretch them and that was definitely not going to happen. Kathy had placed her admirable eyewear near her on the white linen tablecloth as well.

Shasta held the menu and perused it for a moment or two. Upon his request, she replied, "I'll have an orange mandarin salad with walnuts, a side of fresh fruit, and a glass of Pierre water". "Shasta, are you on a diet?" Kathy asked. She shook her head as she was nibbling on the fresh bread that the waiter had brought to their table before Kathy arrived. Upon wiping her mouth, she remarked, "Girl, no!! I always eat a light lunch when Chris and I have plans for dinner".

The two ladies hung out for another hour or so. They chatted about work, men, exercise routines, and whatever crossed their minds. With their longtime friendship spanning 10 years or so, genuine conversation was never problematic.

Before she could proceed, the phone rang. Both ladies looked down at their jeweled decorated Blackberry. "Hello, this is Ms. Parker." The gentleman on the other end sounded impeccably professional. "This is Bruce from Chez L'Monte on 3rd Avenue. I need to confirm your appointment for tonight. It's a party for 2 at 6:30 p.m. Is that correct?" Shasta was beaming from ear to ear, "Yes, Bruce, that's correct. We'll be there". The two ladies finished lunch and chit chatted for another 10 minutes or so until they each returned to their downtown respective offices.

Tonight was surprisingly not too cool nor too stuffy. It was a great time to be out on the town with that special someone. The ambience in the restaurant was divine. The lights were dimmed ever so delicately. The background music was jazz with no identifiable artist but the melodic sounds instilled a mood of perfection. Shasta was glowing with pride and her ensemble for the evening was ever too captivating. She had on a red and black fitted dress with a slit on the left side with her 4 inch black and red stilettos she purchased this past winter during a girls' only trip to Sax Fifth Avenue in New York. As usual, Chris was stunning in his all black outfit with red handkerchief in his pocket.

The drive home from the restaurant was totally silent. One would think after such a lovely evening especially on their 3rd anniversary, conversation would abound. But, unfortunately this was not the case. As the soft sounds of Kenny G. played on the radio, their fingers managed to find their way to each other's hand and that touch was ever so enchanting.

Back at Chris' home, the two of them sat quiet, almost lifeless and as one being. They were nestled together watching a movie cheek to cheek. One would think they were married for years as they were laughing at the same cues from the drama or similarly in high school as they couldn't part their clasped hands. "I missed you last night baby", Shasta whispered. He said nothing. He didn't even move. "Chris", she said with a slightly louder tone. "I, uh, need my spot tickled. You didn't do it last night". The commercial came on and still nothing from him. So, she did the next best thing. Shasta gave him a slight nudge in the ribs and placed her face in his lap.

Chris cleared his throat and stared sternly in her eyes. "Baby, didn't you leave our comfy bed early this morning?" he asked her. "No, I didn't!!!" she said and she plopped up all in one motion.

Shasta shook her head in utter disbelief. She couldn't believe what she had just heard. Last night, she stayed at her mother's home. "Chris", "Chris", she said more energetically each time. "You know my mom is having difficulty after her dialysis every Wednesday afternoon so I stayed over there again last night. Those 3 hours sessions are extremely overwhelming emotionally, physically, and mentally for her.", she expressed.

Without becoming too outrageous, Shasta stood, wiped her tears and just grimaced at him. This was clearly because the anger and hurt had built up inside her. She immediately moved her shoulder length wrapped hair behind her ears and felt speechless for just a moment. All she could say was, "Hopefully there wasn't someone else in the bed with you this morning since you apparently can't remember I wasn't the one". Without any further comment, she moved to the door, grabbed her black clutch bag, and walked out. Almost instantaneously, she sped off in her pearl white Lexus convertible.

He was just as confused about last night when he had awakened this morning. He had no clarification other than to know for sure she didn't stay over last night. So, what happened? Where did the blood come from? How did his pants get the tear?

After another show or so, Chris left the house and went driving. His gray, shiny, super clean Porsche sped up the street as if he were in a race. Then the unthinkable happened. He yelled out the window. Chris was using words with four to five letters primarily. The men who ran up to the window were leaning in as far as their pants were hanging off. One in particular handed him a beer and he took it and immediately chugged it down. He could hear someone else in the background saying that's Danny. That same guy told his friends whom he was standing near "Don't get that clean ride confused? He doesn't take anything off anyone". As he was parked along the curb, he was chain smoking faster and faster and the smell even bothered Julio who was hanging in his car trying to talk.

The next morning, Chris woke up with an excruciating headache and he was baffled once again. What had occurred? There was a note on his dresser from someone that indicated 'Danny, don't forget to call me. I owe you for sharing the beer and buying me the cigs!!' He was once again confused. Who was Danny and why was there a note on his dresser for him? Now, to add to this muddle of mystification, all he could remember was the disappointing end to his night with his love Shasta. He leaned over and pushed the answering machine. After listening, a tear rolled down his cheek. It was Shasta. She left a message saying that apparently he truly didn't care. She returned after their fight last night and knocked and knocked. But to no avail. She said she even let herself in but no one was home. The final comment was this was the final straw because if you chose to leave home and not come find me this means obviously you didn't care enough to work out our problems. Her words, "it's over", sounded so final. He knew her well enough to know she meant it.

For months, he would send notes, cards, gifts, and letters but she had them all returned. Shasta was a woman of her word. Obviously he had really destroyed something special since their 3-year relationship had ended so abruptly.

Five years have passed and therapy has been successful. Chris hadn't had an immense breakdown in many years. He is learning how to express his feelings and develop a greater understanding of him and his past inconsistencies. Chris still didn't find out how he had gotten the blood on his hands. He yet yearned to have a wonderful relationship. In particular, he missed his connection with that *special* woman, Shasta. Not only was their relationship over, but the friendship had dissipated as well and Kathy, who initially was friends with the both, was unable to reconnect the once happy couple.

Today, Chris speaks to forums about the condition—**Dissociative Identity Disorder**—DID—(also known as Multiple Personality Disorder or alters) which is a psychiatric diagnosis which describes a condition in which a person displays multiple distinct identities or personalities. He is proud to express to the group, "you are not freaks" and your condition is real. He informed them that people with this diagnosis, DID, demonstrate a variety of symptoms and their fluctuations vary widely. He proudly stressed, "the best treatment may be psychotherapy and medications for some and hopefully reconnecting the identities of disparate alters (various persons) into a single functioning identity".

Chapter V

Broken Heart

The birthday celebration was wonderful; Christmas was enchanting, the New Years holidays were magical, so why did Valentine's Day have to end that way? Barbee woke up one morning, made the phone call, and said it was 'over'.

Dale was in shock. His mind was confused and thoughts were wild. He didn't know if he should call her back or just pray. The only thing that he could do at that moment was to sit in his comfortable leather recliner and cry.

After what seemed like hours, he did the only thing he thought to do. He went to the garage and started his 2006 Toyota Camry. This was his back up vehicle but it was the one she preferred as he had met her in that vehicle. She wasn't really into that oversized, overpriced, black Hummer that he purchased his 5th year into his general dentistry practice. So, he definitely was trying to incite sentimental feelings as he thought driving that particular car would cause something else to spark in her. With roses in mind, and questions plentiful, he didn't quite know how to approach the situation but the gentle approach was his plan.

Within moments, the sky opened up. Rain was overflowing quickly and thundershowers were headed that way. His speeding plan was deterred by the obvious; the weather. He slowed down and headed for her home.

Barbee was unaware of his forethoughts. She had left home early that morning and had taken off work that day. She had plans of getting a massage, manicure/pedicure, and going to the movies for some quiet time. "Ms. Thomas, did you forget", said the voice on the phone. The receptionist continued by reminding her that she had an appointment with her oncologist this morning. She had totally forgotten.

Dale got to her home and knocked and knocked. He couldn't let himself in her home because despite their three year on/off relationship, she still hadn't given him a key. He was content with that and had promised to understand as he secretly planned to propose on Easter Day of this year. Although it was only a couple of months away, as of this moment, things looked a little foggy. He walked back to the car in sheer frustration. Where was she this time of morning, he wondered. He was already disturbed as she had broken his heart at 4:30 this morning and now it was 6:30 and she wasn't home. He did the next obvious thing. He called her job while still sitting in front of her home. He knew the receptionist came in early as he called the back office extension. After learning she had taken off today, his heart became even more shattered. She never did anything without at least sending him a text to keep him abreast of her actions.

The appointment went great. Dr. Mormon had given her another clean bill of health. She had been ovarian cancer free for three years now but was continuing to have her regular check-ups. She had longed for a child for at 34 her personal internal clock was yet ticking. She had lost her only child at 26. He, Evan, died of SIDS. She was married to his father who had died just three months later as he was the victim of a random mistaken identity shooting incident.

Barbee frequently spent time at Baby Evan's grave. Even though just 1 month old, she chose to have a funeral and enjoys visiting his gravesite. She never would think she was to be childless and single almost 8 years later.

Three hundred miles away, Michael was enjoying his day. He was a photojournalist by day and an avid exercise buff by evening. He enthusiastically favored working out and staying in shape. He was 47 years old; 6'1" tall, had won several marathons, and weekly wrote a health article for a national magazine. His other allure was his appearance. He was a biracial man who happened to be proud of both his ethnicities. His body was so tuned most people thought he was in his late 20's to early 30's.

"Mr. Tate, you are scheduled to go to Milan to cover the upcoming awards banquet for L-Esseque, one of the most noteworthy publications of the modern day", said the assistant. She worked for Michael and several other photojournalists at his office. He immediately made plans but had to make a phone call first. "Baby, I will be out of the country for a couple of weeks. Our Easter plans will have to be put on hold but we can take a trip to the Bahamas immediately afterwards or your choice. I love you, 'Anne'," he said in the most romantic voice of all. His typical baritone accent wasn't as apparent on the machine or so she thought.

As the sun cleared up, she had cancelled her plans to have a manicure/pedicure but the massage with her favorite masseuse, was yet in motion. Herbert had the most wonderful hands. They were strong and gentle simultaneously. Her choice was the Swedish massage and she truly was in need. Her work as a dentist required immense precision and astute professionalism on a continuous basis. As a pediatric dentist, she not only worked with children but she was involved in many charitable organizations and was active in her church.

While sitting in the car preparing to go see her movie, Barbee took out her photo album. Inside the book, she was reminiscing over her relationship with Dale. She loved looking at the appearance of the two of their skin tones next to one another. They were both biracial; she was Italian and African American and he was African and Hispanic. But he had this interesting allure in appearance and etiquette which was normally associated with a stylish man from Wall Street. There were plenty pictures of him; both alone and with her. She even cried at the excitement they shared on their faces. Without hesitation; she stopped crying and prepared herself to get out of the car. Unfortunately, she accidentally hit the button on her phone and turned it on without notice.

As she was walking up to the movie booth, it rang. Dale was elated that it wasn't going to voicemail anymore and was anxious to talk with her. He wasn't sure how to begin the conversation but he just knew he wanted to talk. After looking down at it, she refused to answer it. He was totally floored and chose to leave just one more message as he had previously left over 30 from 8 a.m. until 2 p.m. (now).

Dale tried hard to focus while at work. After seeing just two patients and realizing he wasn't as friendly as normal he decided to go home as his patients deserved better from him.

Back at home, Dale sat on his couch and looked at the video of him and Barbee. They created it about 18 months into their relationship. He watched and cried and cried and watched. Then, he gathered himself and tried hard to figure out what happened. Then, it struck him. He remembers occasionally being a bit too overprotective, verbally harsh when she worked too much, jealous more often than not, and of course the biggest issue. He was seen on camera kissing a patient's mom. He assumed it had been off but he didn't press the cancel button as he thought. Barbee only noticed it as she was waiting out front for him and it appeared surprisingly on the screen. She kept it secretive but had taken a video of it with her phone. Every so often, he thought she knew as she abruptly decided not to visit his office any longer during office hours. But he never revealed his indiscretion regardless of his own conscience bothering him week after week.

He shook his head. He couldn't fathom the cause of that ironic call he had received this morning. They had been doing so much better. Or so he thought.

By week's end, Barbee closed out all her accounts and finalized loose business ends. She did send personal notes to all her clients making appropriate referrals. The moving truck was coming tomorrow and she was set. With 120 hours past, [5 days specifically], she had managed to avoid any confrontations with her now former mate— Dale and fortunately had continued to avoid his repetitive, numerous messages. She was not only glad but relieved.

"Dr. Joy, I did it. I finally decided to free myself", she said to her psychotherapist. She went on to say she ended the drama of her supposedly perfect relationship. She said she wanted no more and deserved so much better. Dr. Joy released her as a client and promised to make her an appropriate follow up recommendation in her new location if so inclined.

The plane ride was a little over an hour. She had sent her things forward via moving company but she decided to fly. She wasn't up for the long drive. As she walked out the corridor, she saw him. It was Michael. He was her true love that she had missed and was ready to fully dedicate herself to in totality. It began as a friendship but now it had grown emotionally as so much more.

There would be no more long distance calls. There would be no more anticipation of when it was to happen. Barbee and Michael had finally reconnected. The two of them had established a connection during a conference she went to over a year ago. She hadn't cheated on Dale but this was during their on/off stint. Michael was a calming factor for her. During the entire two years, he had never raised his voice at her. He was understanding of her dynamic work schedule and fully supported all the activities that brought her joy. She didn't like juggling her friendship with Michael considering her relationship with Dale. But she was committed to believe she didn't merit the inconsistency of his emotions and wanted something more 'sane'.

Two years later, Barbee and Michael expanded their relationship into a more permanent state. They got married and by her 37rd birthday, she was pregnant. Her baby girl was born one month prior to their anniversary and she was more elated than ever with her life, family, and complete happiness. They decided to name her Anna as it was close to her middle name, Anne, which was Michael's pet name for her.

Chapter VI

The Black Rubber Tire

It was bound to be hot as the news had forecasted 96 degrees this entire weekend. Despite the temperature, the forestry was lovely. The leaves were a beautiful, multi-colored pattern; red, green, and yellow. The grass had a plush thick feel as it felt good between your toes. But the bugs were extremely plentiful; crickets, grasshoppers, and snakes.

The walk down to the river was peaceful. It was a time for Carmelita to be at one with herself. She could sit on the embankment and just think. "Wow", she said out loud to herself. "It is so perfect today", she thought. She was 32, single, and originally from Arizona. But due to the recent death of her favorite grandma, Ma Hattie, she had moved back to the family home in Hattiesburg, MS.

Today, she is down at her favorite spot, 'The River of Love'. Well, that's what she affectionately called it. It was actually a lake near Ma Hattie's house. Out there she and her grandma and grandpa would fish and talk for hours when she was young.

Psss, psss, psss . . . The sound was ever so close. Almost in a blink, the next sound rang out super loud—*POW, POW, POW*. Grandpa had stood up and shot it. The 10' ft gray rattlesnake was no longer slithering towards her body. Its plans were to place venom in her thick, juicy legs. But her grandpa had different plans. He was going to put that thing to sleep—permanently!!! He had tried to reassure her, "Sit still Meenie, I got it". But of course Carmelita couldn't hear those words. All she could do was stand still and cry silently as she learned this tip in a camping trip with the girl scouts many, many years ago. When that gunshot rang out, so did the last moments of that poor, but dangerous snake' life who had purposed to do her harm, or little did it know!! The first shell hit his head and it flew to the east, the second shell entered its mid section and it ripped its body into pieces. The last shot hit its rattle and that sizzle would no longer exist.

But this was just a memory; Grandpa had died when she was 11 but those memories were just as clear and real as yesterday. She actually stood there and cried for a moment. She looked into the sky and said 'Grandpa, I miss you so much. I wish you were here to say Meenie just one more time'. By the time she uttered the last words to herself, she heard a familiar sound that made her grin. It was her stomach growling.

The picnic basket was just 15 yards way. White grapes, juicy strawberries, and mixed melons were ice cold in a small zip lock bag. Because of her OCD (obsessive compulsive disorder), she warmed up the lunch meat; smoked turkey and ham, as well as the bread. This was a bit peculiar some may assume because the food would sit outside and be cold prior to her consuming it. However, she simply refused to eat meat that she knew came straight from the refrigerator and wasn't heated at all. Likewise, she liked her bread to have a certain texture which could only be attained after it was warmed in a microwave. The dasani water bottles were frozen. She could see the ice glacier that stood in the middle of the bottle. Condensation had already begun to take place as the bottles were sweating. But she yet couldn't drink it because the huge icicle kept hitting her lip when she put it up to her mouth.

Almost 2 hours had passed; she glanced down at her watch and realized it was only about 1:30 in the afternoon. Time had flown by. She had already thrown back a couple of small whiting and even larger brim fish. However, she didn't have plans to keep them anyway, but the hobby just was too relaxing to pass up. She wasn't quite sure of the temperature but her big straw hat had been preventing the sun from burning her forehead. There were sweat beads still forming under her hat but this was not as bad as could have been without the tan brim. Every few moments, she would wipe her neck with a paper towel from her yellow bag which was laid against the basket. For just a second, Carmelita realized she had forgotten how different the heat from the South was in comparison to that in Arizona. In Mississippi, she now remembered the humidity could be sweltering and smothering unlike any other. Out there (Arizona); she felt more of a dry sensation as the two climates were totally different.

With fishing pole in hand, songs in her head, and peace in her mind; she noticed something quite unusual. Out in the distance, she saw it. A black rubber tire was floating. Carmelita thought she was seeing things. She hadn't seen anyone and knew she came alone. So, she slowly stood up, refocused her eyes and tried hard to adjust her vision. She desperately was trying to figure out what was approaching her direction. Fortunately, she had 20-20 sight which allowed for greater depth perception. But this was quite unusual especially for this particular lake.

The lake wasn't the type that people frequently littered in. Only occasionally would you hear a lot of complex noises. Sometimes a family may have a party or so out there. Sometimes there would be a few men out there fishing for crappies or brim. But trash and the like wasn't normally seen out here. It was almost always this beautiful bluish-gray color. One could see the heads of fish as they were swimming beneath the clear water. For all these years later, it was still the same.

But she wasn't seeing things. The tire was probably the size that one would envision on a three-wheeler. But it was just an inner tube, or she thought. It was drifting closer and closer towards her. Then, strangely enough, it had something atop. It looked like a puppy.

She had gone from curious to anxious at the thought of seeing this puppy. How on earth did it get there? How on earth did it manage to survive not falling into the water? Why was it in the lake? Did its owner know about it? Carmelita had various questions and of course she apparently had no one to pose them to. Of course, this cute, maybe 4-6 pound puppy sure couldn't talk.

By the time it floated close enough for her to grasp it, she did. She reached down and took it from its home; the black rubber tire. It whimpered but appeared calm when Carmelita stroked its face. She talked ever so gently to it. She hadn't had a puppy since she was 9. His name was Rondo. Rondo was a poodle who had gotten run over by a truck as he ran out the yard chasing a ball. Those fond memories were comforting as she remembered everything about him.

Rondo was black and white. It was probably a mulatto but she wasn't sure. She was too young to truly understand the difference, so she kept saying he was a poodle. Her grandpa had given it to her when she was just 6.

As Carmelita moved near her basket, she wiped the puppy with her extra blanket. She wanted to warm him up for he had been shivering. So, she wrapped him up gently in the blue throw she had brought out there to lie on if she felt so inclined. It wasn't something that she typically did when she would go to the lake. But this throw was given to her by Ma Hattie so she knew secretly she would watch over her while at the lake.

Lunch was good. She decided to turn on the radio which was near her brown basket. While sitting on the brown blanket, she kept looking into the sky because amidst all the sun were perfect billowy clouds. She nibbled on the fruit and ate only half of one of her sandwiches. When she reached back into the basket, she saw the fresh chocolate chip cookies she had forgotten about. They were gooey and soft. Not too mushy but with just the right texture. She even shared her a few miniature crackers with her new little friend.

Stacy took her newfound puppy back to the car with her. She looked at it and said, "I need to name you". It clicked in; she would call her 'Frisky'. She knew that may sound like a cat but she hadn't stopped wiggling since she put her in the blue throw. Due to her excessive friskiness, she had to remove the cover from her for she was afraid she would fall.

When the two of them reached the house, she told Frisky, she had a little work to do. Carmelita was a paralegal for an attorney and had brought some work home. She was hours behind schedule but she needed that emotional break and the lake always provided the contentment she needed when her thoughts and past were all running amuck.

At work the following day, she had a revelation. As much as she liked her new puppy, she should probably find its owner. She was growing attached but was convinced she had already fallen for it within 24 hours and its owner was probably definitely at a lost as well.

Back at home, she took pictures of it and then posted them in the nearby town. She even took out an ad in the local newspaper. It only ran once a week so she couldn't list it until the next day for it to run two days later. This was a bit out of her custom as she was familiar with daily newspapers.

Carmelita and Frisky would have fun. She was already getting adjusted to her. It was eating more day by day and nibbling at her ankles even more. She had already purchased a few treats and had scheduled an appointment with the veterinarian in the area. She wanted to ensure she was healthy.

The veterinarian was very comforting to work with. He checked the puppy and told her Frisky was actually 9 ½ pounds. She had been feeding her well these last two weeks. He asked her, "Carmelita, where did you say you found Frisky"? She initially didn't hear him because her mind was floating. She was thinking back to the magical day when she was having memories of her grandparents at the lake then she found a puppy which reminded her of Grandpa as well. Her insides were beaming with joy.

"Dr. Wiz, I am sorry. I found her just floating in the lake. I was surprised because only God could have allowed her to survive that round black rubber tire without falling", she stated with immense clarity. She went on to tell him that she had posted flyers and an ad in the local newspaper. She said she was beginning to feel more and more like she was hers because no one had called to claim her as of yet.

Dr. Wiz was happy for her and her newfound friend, Frisky. Frisky checked out just fine with the vet and she was very happy. The two of them went to the pet store to secure a new bed and some other items.

While in the store, she was talking with the cashier. The cashier was bubbly and personable. She and Carmelita hit it off well. The cashier told her she was happy for her and her animal. Carmelita went on to tell her she had just recently found her and was beginning to think she would be a permanent part of her family as no one had called to claim her.

After she gave the cashier, Maury, the description, she saw the look of utter shock on her face. "What's wrong", Carmelita asked. Your puppy sounds like mine. I lost mine almost 3 weeks ago. I was down at the lake one day fishing with my brother and as we talked and talked we must have not paid attention. She must have walked too far away and couldn't find her way back for she didn't know the surroundings as I had only moved here about a month ago. Within a matter of moments, she was gone. Tara, my perfect little brown puppy who was a gift from my older brother had disappeared.

Carmelita and Maury walked outside and it happened. Maury looked at her puppy and said it. Stacy was scared. She knew it was over. She had spent her money for nothing. She had wasted her time on this little one just a day or two too long. Tonight, she would go back to spending time with her stuffed animals and empty large home.

Maury said, "Carmelita, this isn't Tara". Carmelita lit up with joy. "Are you sure"? She didn't truly want to extend that conversation too much longer. But she wanted to be sure. Maury reassured her and she was thoroughly excited.

Carmelita drove home with Frisky and after two more weeks went by, she finally decided to take down all the 'Lost Puppy' flyers. Carmelita would now have a new friend to go to the lake with and would now be a part of her life permanently.

Chapter VII

The Traffic Light

Her road rage was shameful. Today, it turned into the unthinkable. At the traffic light, it happened . . .

Just 12 months prior, she was in a good place. She had recently received a sizeable raise on her job, that was fantastic, almost 8%. That kind of raise was unheard of by most. Shortly after that, she had just come back from the Caribbean with her two closest friends, Sharon and Wilma. That trip was wonderful. They all let their hair down and sisterly committed to keeping secret what happened in the Caribbean. It was similar to the adage, 'what happens in Vegas stays in Vegas'.

After going to the store, Haley decided to fix vegan chops, Caesar salad with vegan dressing, fresh cauliflower and broccoli, and iced tea for dinner. Her husband, David was already home. He had a short day at the office as he was the Dean of the Department of Economics at the community college.

Dinner was great. They ate a little early since they had extended plans for the evening. This was easy since they had no children and it was just the two of them. They had tickets to go to a play afterwards, 'Les Miserables' which had finally come to Richmond.

On the way home from the play, both Haley and David were tired. Screech . . . went the tires of the blue Mountaineer. A car had cut them off and David had to slam on brakes. Haley immediately went into a tirade. "If I was driving, I would have hit them. It's not your fault people can't drive sweetie", she said. Her ears were hot, heart was racing, and foot was taping. "If you pull up alongside that car, I will definitely give them a look to make whoever is driving reconsider", she stressed. David reluctantly edged a bit closer. He could see it was an elderly gentleman who was probably lost or confused. Haley didn't care the drivers' age or problem. Unfortunately, her biggest gripe was slow and stupid drivers as she referred to most on the road.

The drive into work the next morning was smooth for Haley. She was an Executive Assistant to the Chief of Staff at Richland Fennimore Hospital. It was the largest burn facility in the Southeast. She took care of all of the scheduling, meetings, and follow-up budgetary issues that arose from each department. She had four persons under her and reported to the most important individual within the hospital administration.

Wilma was an aerobics instructor at Fitness 7/7/7. She worked out so religiously that everyone either loved her look or hated it because she was so toned. Wilma enjoyed also being a fitness coach to some private clients. They were people who didn't have time to work out in a traditional setting. Each of those persons deemed one-on-one training because of their hectic lifestyles. She was definitely accommodating as one individual would pay as much as she made in a week at her regular job.

By noon, Haley showed up at Fitness 7/7/7 to pick up Wilma for lunch. "Girl, I just went off on this weird looking man at the red light just before turning onto Greenwich Circle", she proclaimed. "What happened", Wilma asked with great concern. "He jumped over without signaling. Can you believe him? Not two lights before that I cursed out someone else". Haley had a serious temper when it came to driving and it was quite evident.

As a result of that madness, Wilma drove them to lunch. The two of them had a fabulous time chatting in the car and looked forward to lunch. Sharon, the other part of this threesome, even met them at Ruby Tuesdays. Due to it being Friday, Sharon had a glass of wine at lunch. This was atypical for her. She actually had a problem with alcohol but wouldn't admit it to herself. She drank regularly at lunch, especially when no one was looking. In her private moments, she enjoyed a night cap or two of which she indulged regularly. For her, it was unclear if it was because of her recently losing her father and mother within the past year or simply because of genetics. Regardless, she needed to seek help.

David was a tall man and he was greatly respected by his colleagues. He was 5'11", stocky build, and extremely gentle. He had the most attractive ocean blues eyes and smiled more often than not. With him being the oldest and only male child, he frequently visited his mother on his lunch break as she reared him and his four sisters single-handedly. Because of that in point, he had always admired her strength.

Ms. Patterson, David's mother, eagerly invited David and Haley over for dinner. She wasn't the typical 60-year old with 5 children and 6 grandchildren. She looked great for her age. She had silver hair that came to the middle of her back and the physique of most 30-year old women. She was still working and extremely active. She worked an average 35 hours a week and was involved in several community activities. For dinner, she prepared two separate meals. One was vegan for her son and lovely daughter-in-law. The other one was for her; grilled turkey chops, squash, and sweet peas. Everyone could enjoy the cake as she had learned to prepare it without the fillers that Haley couldn't partake in with her special dietary restrictions.

At home, Sharon sat staring at the classifieds once again. She was having one of those moments. Her MS had flared and the pain in her legs was quite severe. But she assumed her frustrations of being unemployed was at the forefront of her hurting especially today. It had been 5 months, minimal interviews, and still no job. She had tried and tried to secure one by applying in every avenue possible. Her insurmountable attempts had seemingly been for nothing. For to have several degrees and no job, was yet mentally embarrassing and exhausting to say the least. But all along the way, she was trying hard not to lose her mind in the midst of this dilemma because extreme stress would elevate her blood pressure. Due to her friendly personality, her base of associates would sometimes refer her to jobs that were outside of her normal professional arena, but those didn't come to fruition either. Sharon also had a lot of self-pride. She didn't tell her friends that she couldn't afford her medications right now. It was just too much for her. She was surviving off unemployment which was running out and short term disability insurance money which she had privately taken out as well.

Was the drinking because of her physical pain? Was it because she came from a background of alcoholics to include several aunts and uncles? Or was her indulging in the bottle due to her sleepless nights because of her longing to talk to her mother and father again? The two of them had been killed by a drunk driver who crossed the median almost 7 months ago. She had yet to deal with that loss. Sharon was an emotional mess and her physical difficulties were just as tumultuous. What was she to do?

Wilma was probably the most opposite of her friends. She had a relatively balanced, quasi-normal life; stable job, calm demeanor, and her bisexual lifestyle suited her just fine. She didn't discuss her relationships with the two of her friends unless she truly believed there was to be some longevity. Or conversely, the person truly had to connect with her on every level. But she was proud of who she was. She didn't feel ashamed of who she was or anything she did. Most of the time, Haley and Sharon thought she was just confused because she would comment on a sexy man when they were out in public. But only she knew her heart. She truly desired the intimacy of softness on a more connected level but her friends unequivocally wouldn't understand what that meant; so, she maintained their love and respect and didn't desire to change that!!

With today being Haley and David's 5th year anniversary, they both woke up acting like newlyweds. They had a wonderful 18-month romance and it ended with an incredible proposal on the beach of

St. Martin. Now, 5 years later, David was beginning to have feelings of wanting a child. He wanted to reopen that conversation with her but was very reluctant. He thought she would immediately shut down because they had already experienced two miscarriages. Also, she had prior female issues, in particular, laparoscopic surgery due to endometriosis and severe scarred tubes. Her doctor told her that with that type of scarring, it could be potentially difficult to carry a child to term. But David was yet prayerful.

He planned a wonderful evening to include dinner at the most exquisite restaurant in town as he had already sent her two dozen pink roses to her job earlier that morning. Today he didn't even go to work but she was no less excited than he. She had bought him a new suit and sent him a special basket from Incredible Edibles to his job. Unfortunately, to her chagrin, he wouldn't get it until the next day.

That night was magical; as Haley stood in the floor length mirror getting dressed David admired her from across the room. Her brunette hair was pulled back with a gold hair clip; she had on nude lip gloss, and only minimal make-up. With her ivory tone and flawless skin, she truly didn't need it.

At dinner, the two of them received a shock. The maître d' brought over a round basket filled with snacks and other treats. It had been prepared by Sharon and Wilma who had secretly sent it there on their behalf. His mother, unbeknown to them all, had ordered a special serenade for the two of them as well. That night, David even broke his normal strong persona and shed a tear or two.

The following Tuesday, they both slowly and unwillingly emerged from bed. Yes, they enjoyed one another their entire 3-day weekend. "It was great being off yesterday Poo Bear", David said. "I know, baby. We need to do that more often and not necessarily have an excuse such as our anniversary." After an extended shower together, they both managed to get out the house and head to work.

The traffic was extremely hectic today. Little did Haley know prior to leaving home, the local news channel had reported a major traffic accident on the interstate which meant she needed to take a detour to get to work. It was only in the car that she heard it on the radio. So, she quickly decided to go down Troll Lane instead. Up ahead at the light, a car was stalled. It didn't have any blinkers on nor have its hood popped. But the driver was totally oblivious to this kind of courteous behavior. As she approached, she was caught behind him. She blew and blew. The driver motioned for her to go around.

Haley became irritated and was adamant that he was going to move and move now. "Get out the way, jerk." She wondered to herself, why do people who can't drive or have these raggedy cars even come outside? *Honk, honk, honk* . . . She stayed on the horn. If she only went around, like the others behind her, she could have avoided it.

Within moments, the person from that car got out and confronted her. It was a 20-something year old male with a bad temper. Haley didn't care. She thought she could handle anyone and would verbally try. As she was getting out of her vehicle to verbally confront that stalled car driver, the unbelievable happened. Without fully assessing the situation, that 80 degree morning, was becoming more and more distressing. Then, it happened and all in a blink. It was a red car. It sped across the street, probably with the goal of stopping in the median to beat oncoming traffic, but sadly enough it struck her. It hit her so hard she went 15 feet in the air.

In the hospital, as she lay almost lifeless, with tubes hooked to her and machines beeping. Her eyes were closed and she was diagnosed with severe brain trauma and it was unknown the severity of her spinal damage. Eventually David, Sharon, Wilma, and Ms. Patterson all arrived. The physician told them, "she is very critical and surgery is imminent within the next 20 minutes but you can see her for a moment". When they walked in, she tried to blink her eyes but it was truly difficult. "Road rage isn't worth it", she thought to herself. But due to the breathing apparatus, she was unable to verbalize to them. Before they prepped her for surgery, Haley managed to flicker her eyes and look at David. She spoke ever so softly into David's ear who was trying hard to fight back his fear. "This was my fault. I love you all of you and please promise to not do it . . . ." Within moments, the unthinkable happened. She flat lined and died.

Before he left the room, one positive thing came out of this tragedy. The nurse came in and told David she was pregnant. She was five months and hadn't known it. With prayer, the hospital staff managed to save the baby who had to stay in the NICU for almost 4 months. But little Havina survived.

Her memory would not go in vain. David and her two best friends made it their mission to speak publicly about the seriousness of road rage. They knew her last words were that request and they were determined not to let her down.

CHAPTER VIII

Nobility

There was something that resonated sheer respect looking at the two elder men sitting on the porch chatting. Every Saturday morning, they made their way to neighboring porches and shared tales from their military days and discussed how life has changed since their youth. It was quite unique since Mr. Smith was bi-racial (Japanese and African-American) as was his friend Mr. Valerio (Hispanic; German; and African-American). But these two never saw color nor was any other meaningless detail going to hamper their special bond.

In the days of old, racism was rampant. But when men served side by side, all they knew, was the protection of their brother superseded the color of one's skin. As such, this was undoubtedly true for these brothers related by blood or not.

On today, these heroes from of one of the most noted Wars—WWII, recalled vividly the sounds of the gunfire of the enemy. Mr. Smith slightly flinched as they discussed the conversation. "Men, get down", they recalled. He then recalled a constant whirring of ***BAM, BAM, and BAM*** . . . all which sounded closer and closer by the moment. This sound which Mr. Valerio recalled like it was yesterday was definitely surreal. Within a blink of an eye, he felt as if he were swept back in time as he could almost see once again a fellow soldier who had fallen close to them but they were unable to retrieve him due to it being too unsafe. For just a moment, the silence on the porch became deafening. No birds, no trucks, no sirens, no children, no crickets, no noises, just deafening silence!!

"Hey man, are you okay", asked Teddy. He just realized he had yelled too loud and that had probably done something to Barney. Barney leaned back and nodded. "Yep, I am good. As much as I like to talk about those days, I realize how many of our friends we lost and we can never share certain moments with them again." The two said, "Yep", in unison.

Teddy was very protective of his best friend Barney not only because of the brotherly military connection, bi-racial similarities, but also due to their common physical deformities they experienced many years ago. Teddy Smith, now 78, is a partial quadriplegic but most wouldn't know it. He actively wears a prosthetic and is active as most. He participates in the senior version of the Olympics held by the local Veterans Administration annually. He has actually placed in the top 3 finishers over the last 5 years and he plans to continue to do so.

Barney Valerio, now 70, experienced 60% hearing loss in his left ear, has major PTSD, and received a presbyopia lens replacement surgery due to having lost an eye to friendly fire. His eye loss was something they rarely talk about because neither man quite knows how it happens. All they know is one night while walking to the latrine, someone from their camp was cleaning their weapon and it accidentally discharged and it struck Barney in the eye. It immediately imploded. Because of standing that close to him, Teddy lost partial hearing in his right ear as a result of that gunfire as well. That link became a chain that no one could separate.

Unknowingly, hours had passed, and it was dark. "See you next week Teddy," Barney said. Teddy stumbled a bit, got his composure, and then went inside. Barney was slowly easing his way down the ramp that had been built many years ago adjacent to the side of the home.

Barney had no fear in walking home in the dark because all from the neighborhood knew him quite well. Plus, he only lived across the street. Teddy customarily stood in the door and watched as Barney made it inside. They did their usual double flash then held the light on for 2 seconds to ensure they were both safe. Moments later, both porch lights would be off for the evening.

The next morning, Barney woke up spry as usual. He lived with his second wife who he met in Korea. She was actually European/

African-American. Although they always hoped for children, it never happened. But they had pets which required minimal maintenance; turtles and a huge aquarium of tropical fish.

Barney and Estelle did their usual morning walk around the neighborhood bright and early. At 3:30am, he would rise, prepare coffee, prep her newspaper, fix her usual bagel and fruit, and gently kiss his wife of 49 years. He actually met her just 3 months after having met Teddy. Undoubtedly, Teddy was his best man in his wedding many, many years ago.

By 4:30, they were walking out the house. With matching outfits, illuminated walking sticks, and bundles of energy they were ready for their morning routine. It was always special as they walked and listened to either gospel or meditative soothing sounds, like melodic waterfalls.

As they were deep into stride, Barney had a flashback of the day he lost his first wife. He had only been a soldier for a short while. She was the loveliest sight he had seen since he left home. She was a waitress in the local tavern. One dark evening, enemies stormed the tavern and murdered everyone inside. He didn't find out until she was to be buried that she was carrying the child he had hoped for all these years. A single tear drop fell down his face. He refused to sulk as he had a relentless amount of faith. He simply knew God didn't make mistakes. He met Estelle just 6 short weeks after that and they were wed within 3 months of their meeting. Soon, they will be celebrating their golden anniversary together.

Estelle walked rather briskly. Her major health issues occurred in her 30s as she had a hysterectomy due to recurring cysts and fibroids. She also had a partial hepatectomy due to possibility of liver cancer. The cause was unknown. However it was done at the age of 35. Subsequently, she was unable to bear children. Since that time, she has been fitter than most half her age. She eats well, drinks lots of water, takes vitamins daily, and has no health issues deeming medication. For this, she is truly blessed.

By night's end, Estelle did their usual Friday evening routine; she fixed baked fish, homemade French fries, asparagus, and homemade apple cobbler. They customarily ate pretty well but they were realistic that at their age, they deserved to splurge to a degree!!

The next morning, Teddy and his daughter whom he lived with were outside in their garden. Teddy had been a widower for almost 30 years. He was quite comfortable living with his daughter who had three little ones who kept Teddy quite lively. His grandchildren were 4, 14, and 17. Even though they were in totally different developmental stages in their life, they all had a tremendous amount of respect for their grandfather.

The activity of the day was a trip to the zoo. Teddy enjoyed getting out and spending time with his family. He often invited his other neighborhood children whom he believed would enjoy the camaraderie. It also gave him an excuse to ride the train that ran throughout the zoo. Also, he had a true affinity for cotton candy and caramel corn which were his favorite staples at most kid friendly entertainment events.

Although he truly enjoyed his youthful moments, he truly wishes he had invited Barney who never came along because he and Estelle never had children. For some odd reason, he just believed he had very little to contribute to their life without having actually been a parent. Teddy constantly reminded him that his life experience was priceless.

This particular Saturday morning, Teddy made his way to Barney's porch. As the kids ran to the porch asking questions, the men, responded, gave hugs, handed out money, and then reengaged in their talks. It was priceless. Estelle came out with a tray of ginger snap cookies, brownies, and fruit squares. She insisted they only choose 2 of the 6 options before them. The chilled lemonade was set behind the gentlemen for them to enjoy at their leisure. She also proposed to bring out sweet tea but they both they refused that kind offer.

Just within eye sight, they smiled proudly as they saw three little boys playing with toy cars and trucks. They admired how happy they all looked and behaved. Within seconds of munching on their ginger snap cookies, the once peaceful look amongst the kids changed. Although they could hear yelling and threats, they weren't quite sure what precipitated the now raucous behavior. How did the kind and friendly play become so capricious in only seconds? They shook their head, and Barney nodded to Teddy to intervene.

Teddy called the kids over. They stammered and huffed but respectfully made their way over to Barney's porch. "Yes, Mr. Smith", one of the boys said. "Young man, I don't know what's going on, but the friendship that drew the three of you together is much more important than the disagreement that is now interfering with your ability to resolve your difference", he said. Teddy never raised his voice. He didn't stand. He merely spoke and his words resonated in an unrelenting forceful but loving manner.

Barney leaned into the youngsters and asked them one by one, "Do you love your friend? Do you like your friend? Do you want to remain friends?" As they all answered a resounding yes, he asked them to apologize and make up. They did without hesitation. They also displayed their secret handshake which included several pats and claps in harmony.

Teddy smiled and reached in his pocket and gave them each a shiny .50cent piece. Their eyes glistened with joy. One little boy actually acknowledged that he had never seen one before. Teddy told them to hold onto them for 6 months. If they promised no more fighting and arguing he would then give them $50 each for keeping their word. He pulled out a crisp bill so they could imagine what was to come.

"Wow, Mr. Smith really", one of them asked. Teddy nodded and reinforced that to be a man of your word is sometimes all one has. Barney looked at him and said "Oh so true my friend"!!

Teddy and Barney received the biggest hugs and most whimsical handshake of recent days from these three within a matter of moments. It was very reassuring to see the sincerity in their eyes.

Over the next week, the neighborhood seemed quite peaceful and quiet as usual. The sound of fire trucks and police were a rare occasion in their serene community. Tonight was the annual Friday Neighborhood Greet and Meet. Everyone would come together and eat and mingle. The elder relatives like Mr. & Mrs. Valerio, Mr. Smith, a few others routinely sat under a white canopy which had been designated for them. It was set up with large kegs of bottle waters, fresh fruit, and small fans. Luckily it wasn't too hot yet the fans managed to circulate just the right amount of air.

Children were running around playing everything from hop scotch, hot potato, jacks to hiding-go-seek. They were having a blast!! The older teens were sitting together chatting. Some adults had card games set up and some were even nibbling on barbecue which was being prepared by some of the men in the neighborhood. It was truly a good look.

By 9:30pm, teams had rallied to clean and ensure all were moving home safely. The cleanup crew had the streets impeccable within hours. The street lights gave them plenty of security and it helped aid them as they ensured there would be no major residuals left over the next day. Invariably, all were tired but it was a good tired. Without question, from the youngest to eldest, most would probably sleep in late the next day.

As Estelle rolled over, she didn't feel her Barney Bear. She shook her head and walked to the front door. Her suspicions' were right; he was already in his usual spot. She could see the two men up bright and early. They had Sanka, their favorite decaffeinated coffee, in hand, and were sitting peacefully side by side. Invariably, she did the only wise thing to do. She returned to bed for another hour or so.

Today, Teddy and Barney were in comedic form. At this particular time, they were chatting about some familiar moments from their military days. "Hey Barney", Teddy asked, "What is the difference between telling a story to a child and the way men in the military tell stories. Barney leaned back, cleared his throat, and cackled as he begun to answer . . . "Most stories begin, 'Once upon a time'", he replied. But as we recall, they frequently began "Now, you know this shit is the truth because . . ." The two men laughed, laughed, and laughed. It was so pure that the children playing nearby stopped and pointed at how Teddy's teeth appeared to be falling out of his mouth. They actually weren't. Or were they?? Teddy in haste had probably forgotten once again to apply the poli-grip to his dentures. But he wasn't concerned by the bobble in his appearance. He just reached up, pulled them out, and kept talking.

Teddy and Barney sat out there through breakfast although Teddy's daughter brought them something to eat. They would occasionally come inside to cool off and take a gentlemen's break. Then, they would head back out onto their favorite spot. Lunch had come and Estelle undoubtedly came over with sandwiches in tow. Today was just calm and orderly as they were so in sync with their conversation that nothing else seemed to matter. Teddy leaned over and said, "Man, these are truly some good days". Barney replied with, "I wouldn't have it any other way".

Chapter IX

All Cried Out

Cynthia thought she would never remarry. All she did was focused on working. After two failed marriages why on earth would she endeavor into such a draining venture again? But hanging out with her brother, Phillip, and his wife, Yolanda was getting old.

Phillip was determined to find his sister someone. She would kill him if she knew he was contemplating discussing her loneliness with his firefighter companions. But as he drove to work, he was more committed than ever to at least get her a date. If she came over one more night and pulled out that computer after dinner, he just knew he would scream. Just last week, she did it twice as she constantly exhibits her marriage to her work. The dedication is admirable but the excessiveness and lack of having an outside interest was quite apparent. It's not like he wasn't there as he vividly remembers the pain and agony from her failed marriages and the emotional toll that they took on her. He truly understands her apprehensiveness when it comes to dating and her uncertainty about most men. One of her husbands was her college sweetheart but he was a loser. He couldn't keep a job. He gambled away their joint account and pretended as if he had no knowledge. It only lasted about 9 months. The other was to an older man but he couldn't manage to remain faithful which was definitely a problem. This was ended after about 15 months. Phillip basically knew that his younger sister, Cynthia, was a great catch and she deserved better.

Yolanda and Cynthia had scheduled a girls' night for dinner. Cynthia had decided to prepare her famous Alfredo and chicken pasta dish. Yolanda was bringing over her green bean casserole special. This would probably be great bonding time since Phillip wasn't there and they could truly have time to unwind and open up as they generally did with each other.

After dinner, the two, sisters by chance and friends by choice, moved over to the brown sectional which was decorated ever so femininely with orange circular pillows. Yolanda loved her home. One would almost think she had no children because of the glass and cute figurines which were meticulously placed throughout the room. The children had earlier migrated upstairs to the play room only coming down briefly for dinner. How long could they play peacefully uninterrupted was anyone's guess? But when it came down to it, eventually the Wii and having the large 53" TV on their competitive spirits would definitely soon take over. This usually meant the 'adult time' was destined to be limited.

In the midst of listening to the smooth rhythm and blues and friendly "girl talk", Cynthia did her usual. She pulled out her computer and said, "Yodie, please don't tell Phillip, but I forgot to add something to my agenda for the upcoming meeting tomorrow afternoon. It's been on my mind all evening". All Yolanda could do was roll her eyes to the top of her to head and sigh. But of course she understood, her best friend/sister-in-law couldn't help but work.

At home that night, Yolanda and Phillip had a quiet evening after putting the children to bed. He had gone bowling with some of the buddies from work. Prior to his coming home, Yolanda took a nice relaxed bubble bath and found a good book to read.

Upon walking up to the door of Station 31, the alarm screeched and the doors flew open. It was 6:25 a.m. his shift hadn't started yet, so Phillip looked at the other shift in admiration as they scurried to the respective red engines. He looked at the men with the same prayerful sincerity he subconsciously imparted upon each of the shifts. He had worked Shift C for 9 years and held a true connection of trust and respect for each individual. Most would assume all men, but his shift happened to have two females. He, along with the others, held them in high esteem as well. The majority of the people from his shift frequently went out together after work, called one another, and totally enmeshed themselves in being supportive as they could both on and off the job.

Today, Phillip's shift turned out to be a calm one. Other than the call at the end of the previous shift, there had only been one outbound call all day. As a result of such tranquility, he felt at ease with his wife, Yolanda bringing his dinner. Besides, he just wanted to see his wife. His co-workers normally gave him the riot act whenever she would bring him a special meal to the station. He had planned to meet her at the door so she wouldn't have to come inside. Yolanda was 5 months pregnant and glowing. Phillip was proud of Yolanda as this was their forthcoming third child. He was hoping for a son and could already see a little Phillip, Jr. following in his footsteps. Although the couple had not made an actual decision on a name, this was because they both wanted to be totally surprised at his/her birth, Phillip was still secretly thrilled at the thought of a son. His twin daughters were still his pride and joy and had him wrapped around their pinky.

After he saw the black Yukon pull up to the station lot, he heard another firefighter, Randy say, "Hey, Phillip, I think your cheesecake has arrived". The others standing by enjoyed the jesting and chuckled to the good natured joking. "No, Randy, she is bringing key lime pie", Phillip quickly shot back, ending the teasing before it truly got going especially in the fire station on Shift C.

The newest guy at the station was Bruce. He had only been there about 9 months, however, Phillip had been studying him closely, and believed him to be a great prospect for Cynt (his sister). She was a nurse manager and single mother of two beautiful daughters, Angelina and Madeline. Bruce was a hard worker who enjoyed working out during their downtimes. A proud father of a 12 year old daughter, Francesca, whom he eagerly boasts about and joyfully, discusses some of their joint activities. He frequently talked about hanging out with her, taking her to ballet and supervising her softball team on his off weekends with the fellow fire fighters.

The ER was crazy today and being nurse manager held a lot of responsibilities for Cynthia. Today, in particular, was extremely exhausting. The senator was visiting Fairfield for a large rally but unfortunately he had gotten sick in route to the city. He had been having a lot of abdominal cramping and problems with his bowels. Due to an intense schedule, he had overlooked his issues. As a result of his position and the security issues, this demanded a large degree of coverage and rearranging the duties typically of the day for the emergency department staff. This was extremely complicated for Cynthia professionally and personally. She was on edge with him being in the ER because it immediately brought back many memories of which she hadn't focused on for some time. Phillip and Yolanda were the only two persons she had confided in about her relationship with the senator. It's not like he was married, when they dated, for this was after the end of her first marriage, but prior to his election he had been accused of promiscuity which initially stained his reputation with most constituents. This was yet another loss in her life for she had yet to form a friendship with any man since their immense fondness ended in part due to hectic lifestyles. This was almost 15 years ago, but they had maintained a friendship all until she remarried after deciding his lifestyle coupled with hers would be too much for she and the girls.

Despite her hidden secret of the former relationship between her and Senator Roberson, she maintained professional etiquette and decorum at all times. Within the next 15-20 minutes, she ensured everything would run quite efficiently. One of the lead physicians in the ER came in and informed him that he was describing symptoms of diverticulitis. He stressed further testing would need to be done. But he definitely needs to be followed up with his physician after the blood work returned to ensure he doesn't have diverticular, which is a disease of the colon.

Prior to the senator leaving the hospital, Cynthia managed to go in and talk to him privately for a few moments. She tried desperately to reinforce the importance of him following up with his physician when he returned home. His discussion was yet off track from his health. He apologized for breaking her heart and expressed his greatest well wishes that one day she would find a man who deserved someone as special as she.

Almost 2 hours later, the phone rang at the nurses' station. It was Madeline's teacher, Ms. Woods, who had called to share Madeline she was having a difficult day and she needed to have a meeting with Cynthia on Monday to further discuss her difficulties. Cynthia asked if they could meet this afternoon instead because her Mondays are typically horrendous. She agreed and they met about 4:15 in the classroom with Madeline.

At dinner time, Phillip asked his wife about his plan. "Yolanda, what do you think about my trying to hook up Cynt (his fond name for his baby sister)", he wondered with sincerity. "She has been alone for a while and it's time she gets out. All she does is work, exercise, go to church, and take care of my nieces". Yolanda sat quiet for a moment. Then, with her emotional hormones raging, a tear fell down her cheek. Phillip moved closer and said "Baby, what's wrong"? With her head slightly dropped, she said, "She deserves to be happy. She is like a sister to me. I know she looks at us in admiration as we have been married 10 years. We can't predict the future but 'Yodie' is my girl and it hurts that she doesn't have a good man in her life".

By 11:15 p.m., Cynthia finally plopped in bed. All she could do was cry and pray. She regularly meditated throughout the day but today was just so hectic. She told God, "Lord, I truly need a 'CALGON' moment", she exclaimed. She yet hadn't dated in over a year and wasn't particularly interested since most men were either intimidated with her job or irritated with her schedule. Today, she didn't even get her regular 45 minute workout in and this possibly added to her thoughts of feeling overloaded. The running and burning of sweat normally took away some of the complex weight of the day. She felt worse that this morning she had forgotten to go over her baby girl' rules which normally kept her calm. She blamed herself for Maddie (Madeline) was off track today for she had been doing so well as of late.

Just prior to going to sleep, she pulled out her computer for she had forgotten an important meeting the next morning. Normally, she would check her smart phone for meeting reminders but the day was a bit much. She had two outside meetings on tomorrow and one involved a committee which she was leading. She was insistent on always being prepared, so she had to ensure all information had been forwarded to the committee parties and her co-chair knew her responsibilities as well. In particular, this was the third year in which Cynthia was serving on various committees within the hospital and community. She was headed for self-destruction if she didn't take a break soon. By morning, she prayed, cried, and did a quick 5-minute stretch work out to begin another tedious day.

Angelina and Madeline were best buddies. They were 11 and 8 respectively and despite being in different developmental stages, they still got along extremely well. Angelina was a straight 'A' student but Madeline was quite the opposite. Maddie, her nickname by most, regularly received mostly A's and B's with an occasionally 'C'. She had ADHD which caused her talkative spirit to frequently overtake her behavior. Her hyperactivity actions had honestly calmed down from the prior 2 years. Cynthia's nursing skills coupled with her intense research about her baby girls' condition, ADHD, had given her the tools to cope with her daughter in a positive and supportive manner.

Meanwhile, Phillip decided to just make the call to Bruce this morning. This was his 24-hour off day and he was going to use his convincing measures to try and get a date for his sister. His gut hope is that he could get her connected with someone to take some of her emotional and mental stress away.

Bruce arrived within the hour. Phillip had indicated he needed help with his lawn and had told him his tractor had broken about 10 minutes ago. He knew Bruce had a lawn service and may be eager for the additional work. During this time of sweating in the intense heat, Phillip mustered up the confidence to say it. "Hey man, I know you aren't married. My beautiful sister deserves a nice man like you and needs to go out on a date. Uh, this is awkward but do you think you would consider calling her?" Bruce stood in shock. "Sure". After blowing a sigh of relief, Phillip felt like that weight was now off his chest.

While at home, Angelina and Madeline were chilling out as they usually did on Saturday mornings. Madeline was playing with her dolls and singing songs to herself. Angelina was gossiping on the phone with her school buddies. Her favorite friend was Francesca, who lived between her grandmother and father, as her mother had died when she was born. Francesca's father was a fireman and she and Angelina frequently shared stories considering her uncle, Bruce, was one also.

Leaf Middle School was smaller than they knew. Angelina and Francesca were classroom buddies and they regularly were asked to participate on the same team projects. Francesca's grandmother was typically the one who had seen the girls together but was unaware of their soon to be connectedness. She would regularly bring snacks to the classroom and give the two of them a little something different and special from the others. Who was Francesca? Francesca is Bruce' 12-year old daughter and she is the apple of his eye. In particular, she was smart, beautiful, and well-mannered. She had mid-length hair and exuded perkiness as she was almost a preteen child who adapted well to most surroundings. If anyone could have a daddy wrapped around their finger, it was she. Francesca and Angelina had a blast together but little did their parents know they were already friends and this was one less connection to be made. They loved the same colors, musical artists, and dreamed of similar professions upon graduation from college.

That morning, Yolanda proposed an idea to Phillip. All day she had thought about having a barbecue and inviting who else, but Bruce and Cynthia. Phillip was eager to participate in this plan since he was determined the two of them should meet. "Tonight is going to be a blast he leaned over and told Yolanda; then placed a big juicy kiss on her petite lips".

By 6 p.m., both Phillip and Cynthia had arrived for the barbecue. As Phillip was walking up with the drive way laughing his daughter, Francesca, it was truly apparent to any onlooker the pride he held for her. Almost instantly, Angelina called out, "Francesca, what are you doing here", she asked. Francesca ran over and embraced her good friend and said I am here with my daddy. The two of them began chatting and the adults all looked in utter surprise.

By mid-October, they had been on several dates and all was well. The families had met. Children were bonding. Lives were gelling. So, Cynthia had a bit of skepticism. She called Yolanda and said, "Yodie, be honest with me, please sis. What could be wrong with him? Do you think he is gay? He hasn't tried anything with me and just continues to be extremely polite". Yolanda laughed and laughed until the unthinkable happened. Her water broke. After 17 hours of intense labor, little Phillip Jr. made his arrival to the world.

Bruce and Phillip had formed a closer connection as well. They joined the other guys at the fire station on a boy's only trip to Las Vegas. Surprisingly, they were all very good. They did go to a few shows, Patti LaBelle was performing and Sinbad was also a big hit for them. This trip was just 3 months after the baby was born. Some would think he would need to be home with Yodie, his pride and joy, but she seconded his need to go away for this boy's only trip. The last 3 months had been draining at the station as they had lost 2 members to fires and they needed a reprieve from the norm.

Back at home, Madeline was having a birthday party (November) and all the children were inside. This became a little inconvenient because all the activities had been planned for outside but it was too late to cancel. Besides, Madeline would have thrown a huge fit despite the fact that her medication had truly balanced her temper for the most part. The original plan was to have everyone relegated to being outside but surprisingly it snowed. This was California and snow was definitely not an expectation by anyone.

Within the next 12 months, Cynthia and Bruce had gone on several dates. Some even included the girls. They had taken two out of town trips with them; one to Six Flags in Atlanta and the other to the beach in Florida. It didn't take them long to figure out that everyone enjoyed traveling and relaxation was much needed by all. The next trip was for the two of them as Bruce had fallen in love during the last 18 months, and only wanted to bring Cynthia eternal happiness. Cynthia had also found an ability to trust again as this was the biggest reason why she intentionally chose to close herself off from even attempting to date prior to Bruce. She secretly continuously told herself she owed her brother, Phillip, a huge thank you for the happiness she had begun to experience. This was in part due to his love for her as well.

By the following New Years Eve, after 2 years of dating, it finally happened. Bruce proposed and Cynthia said yes. They were in Paris looking into the sky holding one another. Fireworks were bursting vividly in the sky and now that same vigor had another opportunity for two people deserving happiness.

Chapter X

Motionless

PART I

Yes, just 90 days to the day, 46 year-old Ramona Parks still can sense the oddness of what happened. Can she explain it? No!!! But was it real??? Definitely so and she is just now beginning to retake some level of control of her life again.

As she stood in the hallway of her beautiful 5 bedroom home, Ramona was totally motionless. It's as if she were temporarily swept away in a time warp. Her heart didn't appear to beat, her eyes didn't appear to blink, the day didn't exist, and time was just a mere word. It all happened in a glance as her eyes caught the calendar—February 10th. If she were to utter a word, it would be *'swoosh'* for it all raced back as if it were yesterday. Her mere mind remembered the holidays of recent were truly not a time for celebration. This was especially true because of what she had gone through as of late!!! But her tear ducts could produce no more tears.

Ding dong. Ding dong. Ding dong. This was the sound that snapped her out of the trance. Internally, she was glad to be able to shake it off. The tall, grandfather cherry oak clock had been in her family for many years. This was one of a few items that she managed to keep upon losing most of their family's keepsakes in a family fire at the age of 17.

Ramona traipsed down the stairs ever so freely. She was blessed to have few ailments. She had no major illnesses. She took no medicine on a regular basis except for a multivitamin. She drank plenty of water. She wore minimal makeup. She minimized drama in her life and meditated regularly. If one were to look at her, most would assume she still looks like she is in her 20's. Her secret is simple. She takes impeccable care of herself. She grew up in a home with her parents and elders taking many medicines due to high blood pressure, diabetes, and arthritis. Quite to the contrary, she was convinced it wouldn't be her. She was fit and definitely in shape. Although a little heavier than she would like, her doctors approved of her current weight but her preference is to lose about 10-15 pounds over the next 3 months. She worked out 4-5 times a week; bicycling, jogging, yoga, weight training, and frequent massages were all part of her scheduled responsibilities to herself. To be honest, it showed. This was something she took great pride in but she was modest in this area of her life as well.

PART II

"Umm, it smells like rain today", she said. Ramona reached down and picked up her Persian cat, Calla and hugged her lovingly. Calla and Ramona have been a team for almost 7 years. Calla was a rescue pet. The information from the pet shelter was that she had been found abandoned under a house with a broken leg and her tail had been snipped in half. But, Ramona, only saw her as beautiful and unique. She strolled ever so patiently through the corridor of the shelter aisle by aisle. After almost 10 minutes of looking at various animals and speaking to one after the other, she stumbled upon the most beautiful grayish-blue piercing eyes. The sign on the cage said **'7 DAYS UNTIL THIS PET WILL BE SHIPPED TO A NEIGHBORING COUNTY FOR ADOPTION'**. Her heart immediately dropped as she fell for the beautiful eyes of this little kitty.

Ramona had been looking for a pet for the past 6 months prior but just couldn't find one that spoke to her the way she had hoped. She was childless, single, and to date all alone in her big home. Now was the time. The name on the cage didn't resonate with her, "Sadie". So, from personal studies, she recalled the name 'Calla' which is Greek for beautiful.

The day she left the shelter with Sadie, who she had just remained Calla was one of pride and utter joy. She took her to the local pet store and shopped for her. She got her the cutest little bed and made sure it was organically healthy for her. As a child, Ramona had allergy issues. But as an adult she was blessed to be totally healthy. She wanted to ensure her cat was bringing no new germs or potential allergens into her home. She spent almost 30 minutes speaking with the pediatrician in 'Pet Sync" asking question after question. Of course, she received a clean bill of health from the shelter. But, for her own peace of mind, she just wanted to make sure Calla would be well; otherwise she would do whatever it took to get her the best care.

PART III

Calla jumped off her soft cushy bed and ran up to Ramona and stroked her ever so delicately with her tail. Ramona knew immediately it meant she needed to go out. Calla had a unique ability to not use the kitty litter box that was set up for her near the pantry in the kitchen area. She would frequently use the door panel to let herself out during the day. Ramona felt confident in this method because there was a slim chance someone would be able to break into her home which was in an extremely exclusive area of the city and very well secured. Many years ago, she had cameras installed throughout her home as Jacque and Kaitlyn had suggested it particularly because Ramona insisted on being single. They could never figure out how she hadn't found the right person.

As they walked onto the porch, Ramona was so glad that she had a day free to herself. This was her day to allow her body to recuperate from exercising and let her mind rest from her work. As a psychologist, Ramona took her work quite seriously. So, she purposely chose to have one day off during the week, Thursday.

As Ramona sat in the big wicker chair on the porch, she felt utter peace as it's been a while since she could sit, relax, and think in an unburdened manner. However, it was just 3 months ago to the day that she lost her 3 childhood friends back to back. That was a dark moment that she thought she would never survive. But fortunately she did.

Jacque had gone skiing for the first time in Aspen. He had been invited there with some attorney friends as they had just won the biggest case of the quarter. The case involved one of the hottest murder-suicide cases of the past 20 years in their midsize town of Murfreesboro, TN. Murfreesboro was traditionally known for MTSU and other notables such as the Tennessee Miller Coliseum and TSSAA state championships for football.

The accident itself had been so unusual. Most frequently someone would be found plunged off a trail in this beautiful resort. But not in his case, Jacque always did things in high fashion. He had accidentally fallen off the ski lift as it had ascended up in the air to round the ski hill. This 30 year old lift had never had any malfunctions prior to now. Honestly, he and his buddies checked the safety report upon arriving to the lodge just a few days ago. All indications were everything was well. He was all alone as he was hoping to pose for pictures via the attached camera. He was moving about but was promised it was safe to do so. He plummeted surprisingly to his death head first but he hit a huge rock which was embedded in the snow. It was devastating for all.

Many years ago, he was a very successful football player both in high school and college. Ramona, Kaitlyn, and Brandy had all tried to convince him to accept the wonderful offer he received from the Canadian and NFL league. But he chose to not leave them. They were his family. Jacque lost both his parents by the age of 6 as they went on their first vacation since his birth. Oddly enough, they were killed in a freak trail derailment. Ramona's grandmother stepped up and cared for him for all those years. Back then, legality was a mere technicality. This was the benefit of coming from a small town. Kaitlin and Brandy's parents were equally relevant in his support and mentoring.

Jacque and Ramona actually met at the end of their 5th grade school year. They were both still awkward and just began to understand that boys and girls could actually be friends. They would occasionally tell people "we are just buddies" whenever anyone would ask. It just flowed off their tongues.

Jacque and Ramona frequently met after his games for a regular match of chess. "Check mate", she said. She leaned into and said "I got you again". Jacque grinned just momentarily but quickly snapped back into stoic mode. He wanted to get her as she had just won their last few matches. But he knew he regularly dominated in this sport.

Ramona wasn't big into 'girlie activities' like cheering or modeling. But with her best friend by her side, she would venture to try anything at least once. She did run track. It didn't take her long to figure out that she had talent. This is where she and Kaitlyn dominated. They were utterly glad because the two girls were almost sisters. Or so they thought. They both were tall in statue and developed very slowly.

Kaitlin was actually adopted but this didn't deter her from feeling totally whole in her home. She was shipped from foster home to foster home until the age of 8 when she moved near Ramona. "Ramona, isn't that an odd name", Kaitlin asked. Ramona was already aware of Kaitlyn's unique family situation so she was very gentle in responding. "No, Ramona was my great aunt's name and my mother named me after her. I kind of like it", she said. After that uncomfortable moment, the girls quickly found more likenesses in each other than not.

Brandy was different than both Kaitlyn and Jacque. Eventually the three of them would be inseparable. Jacque was the big brother that Kaitlyn and Ramona never had. Brandy entered their high school days and immediately felt like an outsider. She was almost 250 pounds, 5'1, freckled face, with brunette hair. The most radiant thing about her was her confidence. She walked into any room and immediately garnered attention. This was simply phenomenal.

Brandy enrolled herself in the homecoming court of their incoming senior season. Of course she knew no one. But the one thing that no one could take was her ability to garner friends with her impeccable personality. She came into the school with a 4.2 GPA. Her family moved to Forrest City, Arkansas from Franklin, Kentucky where she had been in private school for the past 5 years. Her mother and father were both dentists and they had a dual practice. But due to the plummeting economy, it took a turn for the worst. So, they moved to Forrest City to be near Mr. Branford, Brandy's paternal grandfather. He had been declining in health for the past 3 years. His initial diagnosis of liver cancer had been a secret for many years. But seemingly all of a sudden he was unable to control his diabetes and blood pressure so her Brandy's parents made the only decision possible; to relocate to care for him.

After just three days of talking, Brandy became the 4th part of the once triangle with Ramona, Kaitlyn, and Jacque. Brandy now had a team to support her on her quest to become homecoming queen. Ramona and Kaitlyn had no interest in vying for this role. Of course, Brandy asked after she began her new friendships with the girls. She even told them if one of them wanted to run she would pull out of the competition. She was only doing this to add to her collegiate application. She was always told how important it was to have extracurricular activities throughout school.

At the homecoming dance, Jacque managed to be named MVP for his athletic prowess. He was a stellar quarterback. His personal cheerleaders were his two best friends. His teachers all admired how he protected and respected the girls. Even more surprisingly, he escorted the three girls because they all chose to turn down potential dates. This was quite usual as their bond was more vested than any dates from the home town boys in Forrest City.

Brandy was named homecoming queen. It didn't take long for the smartest girl in school, Brandy, coupled with the two friendliest girls to foster a strong coalition to help her win election. This was a time when girls were honestly joyful for their female friends and not egotistical about their accolades.

PART IV

Within them all being 45 years old, as they were all within months of each other, the perceived leader and big brother, Jacque called for a special trip. Now, was definitely a good time. It had been a while, specifically, about 5 years since they had gone away so taking a cruise appeared to be in order for all of them.

Over the past few years, they had moved away from close proximity but yet still close enough to get to one another within 45 minutes to an hour by plane. They didn't move away from one another because of pride or superior behaviors exhibited by some when they professionally elevated. But this quad of friends; a lawyer (Jacque), psychologist (Ramona), model (Brandy), and sales professional (Katilyn) all were in understanding that no matter what they would never lose their closeness. They text and Skype each other at least 3-4 times a week.

Brandy had been married and divorced. She had sadly enough lost her then husband and children in an unfortunate car accident. A drunk driver took out the lives of her twin 3-year old boys. Her husband, Ralph, had gotten out of the car after the accident and tried desperately to reach them. He was unfortunately killed by another oncoming car. This left Brandy motionless for almost a year. Her modeling jobs had ceased and expectedly so. Ramona, Kaitlyn, and Jacque had gone to be by her side. They reminded her that regardless of the divorce papers being served to him the day prior to the accident she didn't need to put a title to their relationship. Brandy and Ralph had been an inseparable pair since college. Of course, Jacque walked her down the aisle. He was the only male in her life that could represent her at such an occasion.

Kaitlyn frequently went on missions abroad. It was just in the last 3 years that she elected to take a job in the states and allow herself to be used to serve the good of her people closer to home. She enjoyed the travels but her lupus frequently gave her quite difficulty. This was particularly problematic in foreign countries as her medications were often hard to acquire.

PART V

"Ms. Parks, you have an emergency phone call", Sam said. Sam was Ramona's assistant who had been with her for the last 10 years. Sam was tall, brawn, and extremely articulate. Most wouldn't imagine how a hunk of a man who appeared to walk out of any magazine would want to be an assistant. But to him, it was a natural transition. He moved from Sydney, Australia to the states because he was simply tired of being only a male model. Modeling was fun but I guess after watching his sister travel overseas since the tender age of 6 convinced him it's sometimes better to use your brains than appearance.

"Hello", she said. Ramona just flopped to the floor. Sam ran to her side. "What is it Ms. Parks", he questioned. Ramona could only whimper. It's Jacque. He is . . . Ramona then passed out.

Brandy and Kaitlyn immediately flew to be with Ramona. Although they all loved Jacque, Ramona's relationship with him was a little different. He protected her from bullies, guided her through poor relationships, and listened in the early morning hours when she had no one else to be there for her. Jacque and Ramona never crossed any borders with one another. Not even once. They were the epitome of male/female true friendships.

As Brandy and Kaitlyn worked to get Jacque flown back closer to them, they knew Ramona was in no position to make decisions. They knew despite Ramona being extremely strong in the board room. She was a softie when it came to those she cared for. Her sister-brother relationship with Jacque was simply special. So, they relied heavily on Sam, her assistant, to manage a lot of the particulars of the funeral and proceeding events as they related to Jacque.

As Brandy was preparing to go back home, she had still yet to reveal a hidden secret to her sisters. In their mind, their friendship was more like a sisterly bond because they never held secrets. Or so they thought!! Today, being Thursday, Ramona's favorite day of the week, the ladies were truly enjoying their time together. Popcorn and beer were on the menu for the snacks for their last evening together. Kaitlyn had a flight scheduled for the next day. Brandy was actually preparing to stay an extra week to help Ramona. Even though Ramona was typically an A-personality and kept her house impeccable, she just couldn't find it in her to maintain the usual precise manner that she preferred. This was only as late since Jacque had passed. Ramona snickered to herself as she recalled being called a 'miser' by Jacque and Kaitlyn as they knew she could afford to have someone come in and care for her home. But in her mind, why would she as she is there alone and can maintain her home on her own?

"Brandy, what are you doing in the bathroom", called out Kaitlyn. We have to play at least one game of gin rummy before bed. It was totally quiet. Ramona thought Brandy was simply upstairs crying or praying again as she would frequently shut down since his death. But in her gut, something felt different.

Ramona went upstairs and found Brandy lying in the bed holding her head. "What's wrong sweetie", she asked her. Brandy finally confided in her and said I have HIV and have been positive for years. Tommy gave it to me and that's why I divorced him. I loved him but I told him it wasn't fair that he loved me too little to be honest with me. Ramona stood motionless and didn't know what to say. She wasn't afraid to touch or hug Brandy. But she didn't know how to respond. She thought they held no secrets. Now, this was bigger than a secret.

Ramona told Brandy she was going to prepare a hot bath for her so she could relax. She reminded her that their love could help her get through this. Brandy just couldn't share where she really was mentally with all of this. Honestly, Brandy was so depressed and just couldn't shake it. But Kaitlyn and Ramona were totally oblivious.

After an hour, Kaitlyn went upstairs to check on Brandy in Ramona's overstuffed tub. The marbleized, over-size tub was simply grand in appearance. But Ramona's meekness would never allow anyone to know she lived so well. Kaitlyn saw the unspeakable. Brandy had apparently taken too many of her Truvada, her HIV medicine. She wasn't moving or breathing. Kaitlyn couldn't scream nor cry. She just flopped to the floor.

Once again, Sam stepped in. Sam was surprisingly good at sensing when Ramona needed him either at work or home. She rarely talked about how he had the door panel for Calla built as Ramona just mentioned it one day in passing. Sam had no personal interest in his supervisor, Ramona. He just held the utmost respect for her. His knocking on the door tonight had a remarkable, eerie timing to it.

As Ramona went to the door to let Sam in, she could hear faint sounds from upstairs. She couldn't make it out but her gut just told her to move quickly. But Sam insisted that she stay downstairs. He was right.

Sam ran without haste to the upstairs level. The spiral case was a little difficult to run up but surprisingly he made it look easy. He went from room to room and found nothing. Then, he saw them. He approached Kaitlyn and just touched her hand. He leaned down and allowed his ear to listen for breath sounds from Brandy. It was quite apparent. She was gone.

As Sam went back downstairs to find Ramona, he saw her holding her phone up. Brandy had recorded a message for Kaitlyn and Ramona and sent to her via phone recordings. Ramona was in awe and she was at a loss for words. She is gone she said when Sam walked into the room. Sam looked down at her and confirmed, "Yes, she is".

Ramona and Kaitlyn had just undergone two deaths in less than two weeks. How on earth would they go on? Kaitlyn and Ramona vowed to not go longer than 24 hours without hearing one another voice. They just knew they would need each other even more.

Kaitlyn went back home within a week. She was a successful sales consultant with a top pharmaceutical sales company. She enjoyed being able to get out and meet various doctors and introduce new products. This job brought her great joy. But her lupus yet had its spurts.

The following month, Ramona had to go to a conference in Chicago and Italy. She was well respected in her field and frequently tried to diversify and elevate her professional base. So, during this time, she was unable to connect with Kaitlyn. This didn't change the fact that she thought of her frequently, but the direct communication was halted. Ramona's two attempts at texting her from Italy were unsuccessful. Or so she thought because Kaitlyn didn't respond.

On the way back home, Ramona decided to go to Colorado where she knew Kaitlyn had been. Kaitlyn had been scheduled to go to a huge expo and present and Ramona was going to surprise her. Upon her arrival, Ramona was told by her peers that they hadn't seen her in 2 days. According to Ben, Kaitlyn's colleague, he hadn't been able to reach her. Ramona immediately became worried. She instinctively checked her email. It was there that she had missed a message. Kaitlyn's doctor had tried to reach her and sent her a message to contact the hospital.

Ramona knew it was going to be well so she didn't panic. She just followed the information left her by the doctor and met them at the hospital prepared to receive new information on how to care for Kaitlyn and her Lupus. Ramona didn't want to be astonished, just in case, so she contacted Sam so he could meet her. She reminded him to access their business account for his travel expenses.

The two of them arrived at the hospital at the same time. Ramona thought this was the last place she wanted to be. In her mind, she thought, this is just 45 days into losing Jacque and Brandy. All she could focus on was that she had just buried two friends and now the last one of the four of them is sick. She just knew it couldn't be real. But this surreal experience took her for an emotional toll as when she walked in she saw Kaitlyn hooked up to machines. Ramona walked up to Kaitlyn and tried to remain calm and optimistic. She didn't know what to say other than "I love you". Kaitlyn nodded and removed her oxygen mask and spoke just a few words. "Re Re, (her pet name for Ramona), my white blood cells are failing me. I can't produce healthy red blood cells either. I held on until I could see you", she said. Within moments, she flat lined and Ramona stood motionless and a tear dropped. It was just too much.

PART VI

The next few weeks were hard. Ramona didn't work or eat. Ramona barely took a bath or shower. She definitely didn't work out. All she could do was sit and stare. She was in utter shock. The 3 people whom she loved most, outside of her biological family were all gone. She had already lost her family early in life and now this was simply unbelievable. Words couldn't express her thoughts or beliefs. But, she did the only thing she knew to do, she turned on a gospel station and she allowed herself to release the tears. She allowed the music to minister to her spirit. This was the beginning of her cleansing and healing process.

PART VII

Ramona sat and wrote in her journal. Sam and other coworkers had just left. But, she chose to be alone. It's typically unusual for a psychologist to ask for help. She was no different. This wasn't because she thought of herself as being too good. Conversely, Ramona wasn't the type to be conceded having the impression that no one was at her level professionally. She just needed time.

As she laid in her California king bed, Ramona began to think no more. The rampant thoughts had ceased. The bad memories had stopped. The crying spells had dissipated. The inability to articulate her feelings had halted. In simplistic terms, she was feeling 'lonely'. Loneliness is a natural and normal emotion especially after a crisis such as a loss she frequently told her clients. It will take one step at a time for the pain to go away. Her once painful motionless moments would have to cease as she would get wrapped up in her abysmal thoughts.

Ramona decided to confide in one of her business partners, Paul. She had known him for a while. She greatly respected him and chose to use a male for professional consult to dissect her recent agony.

With almost 2 years of therapy, hundreds of hours of patiently listening and divulging inner thoughts, Paul turned out to be the best thing for her. He helped her process all of her thoughts, feelings, and losses. As they concluded her therapeutic professional capacity over 3 months ago, Paul took a chance and asked her out as a friend. She was quite reluctant as usual. But in the pit of her being, she knew she needed someone other than Calla to spend meaningful time with as she was honestly a good, heart working woman who deserved and needed to smile again. It was just time for her to step out of self and share some time with someone even in a friendly capacity.

PART VIII

Within moments, Calla ran back upon the porch and she could see her favorite person, Ramona in a deep trance. She leapt onto her lap, gave her a gentle snuggle, and hissed at her owner. Ramona rubbed her eyes, looked down and smiled with happiness. She was beginning to recapture the individual within self she thought was lost forever. Her memories of late were not so good but the overall thought of her best friends gave her joy as their love will live within her heart forever. The newfound relationship with Paul was something else she craved to savor.

CHAPTER XI

Humor Untold

As Bob Crowe, a well-known writer sat in front of his laptop generating his 5ᵗʰ top selling novel, he so desired to finally put a story out which depicted the years of comedic humor between he and his longtime friend Jean. She, being almost 30 years his senior, was closer than most to him.

Bob could never repay Jean for who she was to him. She was the sister he never had. She was the mother he had wished had borne him. She was the cousin who he knew he could tell all of his deepest secrets. She was the friend who judged, critiqued, supported, cheered, and loved him greater than all. To his credit, she felt the same.

The two of them met many years ago when they were both parties in a bus accident. She was the driver and he was one of the witnesses/ rescuer. It was quite unusual for her to befriend a mere stranger but after this horrendous accident she truly felt a natural kinship in their initial encounter. But he was unusual than most. Bob had such a gentle approach, that it was almost inevitable that she should reciprocate his kindness.

Prior to today, in Bob's everyday dealings; he gingerly wrote local and internet blogs to complement his professional writings. He was well known for his impression of a small kitten that he would put on the right corner of his writings. He never explained it but apparently he had some hidden connection.

During Bob's monologue at book signings, he frequently would mention that he began writing because of two primary reasons. One was because he enjoyed the explosion he could create in print when he wrote and the second was the commitment he made to his late mom to be diligent in his penmanship. This genuinely won over the respect from many. He would always get many laughs when he mentioned he went through job after job but nothing ever felt right. Some of his jobs included being an account executive for a newspaper, owner of a yogurt food chain, Professor of the Science department at a well-known university, and Art Director for a television station. Some of his friends thought it was odd that he had 4 degrees but was never content with any of them. Then, with less than $25 in the bank, he pulled out a pen and paper and began expressing himself in black and white. He didn't know for sure how to make it happen but was committed to trying and succeeding.

What he never told the general public was the other part of his truth for he didn't want sympathy. He was forced to retire early due to having severe PTSD. But his decision to become an entrepreneur was vastly of his own doing. He loved the freedom and openness he shared in the novels he had printed thus far. He believed in creating something for oneself and establishing your own worth.

From youth to adulthood, irrespective of therapy, he never totally healed from the tremendous loss of his mom and sister. They both accidentally drowned due to a horrible rainstorm. To date, he rarely discusses it but his mother was in a hurry to get his younger sister, Annie to tap dance rehearsal. It had been raining ferociously for the past 2 weeks. She dropped him off at home and asked him to lock the doors and complete his homework. She promised to return by 6:30p.m. It was about 4pm and she hadn't listened to the meteorologist report from her favorite station. It had been reported that a flood was just 2 streets from their home. Her usual route was to go in the direction of the predicted flood. Upon her approaching the street, she could see the water, but had underestimated the depth of the water. Unfortunately after only going 10 meters into the water, her car became overtaken. She couldn't do anything and before she knew it the water had flooded the car. Because of all the rain, it took almost 45 minutes for responders to arrive. Both she and her daughter died due to a lack of oxygen and drowning. Just shortly after leaving their home, she sent Bob a brief text reminding him to complete his homework and to watch his penmanship for people will always judge him based on how and what he writes. Those words stuck with him forever even though he was only 10 at the time. To this end, sadly enough, his father had died at his birth. His dad was recklessly speeding to the hospital after hearing that his mother was in labor. He assumed it was safe to proceed through a red light as it was almost 1am in the morning. She worked at the hospital so her co-workers called him and asked him to meet her as her labor had progressed quickly. Despite being just 10 yards away, two red Dodge Chargers were racing and didn't notice the vehicle had just run the light. All three individuals were killed immediately on impact. Bob never got to meet his father but was proud that he paralleled him as he too was a creative being. He was a musical engineer and had left his mother well prepared to financially care for them. His stepfather, Annie's dad, was killed in a work related incident when Bob was just 5. He was ultimately raised by aunts and uncles until their demise late in his early adulthood.

Jean, who was close to retirement, had limited support systems in this town. After graduation from high school, she began applying for jobs within a 200 mile radius. Her plan was simply to become comfortable financially as she had never been encouraged to attain a college education. But was always told 'you must work' and that's not an option in life. When she was hired as a bus driver, she was so proud because she rode the bus for 16 hours to relocate. In her generation, very few opportunities to attain a college education was afforded to her, so finding a stable job gave her great hope back then.

On that sunny mid-afternoon, Bob was pumping gas at his favorite Shell station when he overheard a male and female arguing uncontrollably outside their car. Without thought, she jumped in the car as did he. The bickering continued as was evident by their rapid head movement and hand gestures. She turned and gripped the wheel. Bob tried desperately to appear to not be spying as their business was obviously private but their behavior made it quite public. As he turned back to glance, he noticed that she apparently was even more miffed based on the way she was sweeping her hair behind her ears and wiping away tears. She then did the unexpected. She pressed on the accelerator and sped into traffic. She definitely didn't look at oncoming traffic as she came off the curb and side swiped the bus. The bus went spiraling into oncoming traffic.

Bob standing within only mere feet of this incident was in awe. His heart seemingly stopped as he was in shock at what he had just witnessed. He quickly stopped pumping gas and began flailing his arms as if to garner the attention of others. His immediate response was to run into the street to see what he could do to help. But someone not too far away, called for him to hail to the speeding fiery black pin-striped two-toned Ford Mustang that was approaching him just as he was to step off of the curb. If nothing else, for the people on the bus needed immediate attention, he had to do something. He and other passerby drivers jumped into action. They all ran to the various individuals to see who needed the most assistance. He felt even more confident in his ability to be a Good Samaritan as he was being aided by others doing the same to relieve the agony and mixed emotions of persons a part of this debacle.

Sara, the female driver of this entire mess was ranting and raving even as the paramedics were putting her on the board to immobilize her. The onlookers were in disbelief as it was obviously her fault. Everyone immediately began to proclaim that alcohol had to be involved. Otherwise no one could be that disconnected from something which could cause such devastation to so many individuals without lack of regard for others lives. Heads were shaking and verbal comments were no longer silent as if to give her an indication that she had no cause for her improper behavior. She wasn't affected by their opinions. She was just in her own mode.

When Bob ran onto the badly struck bus, Jean immediately asked him, was he there to save them. He was a little taken aback as he was surprised that she hadn't gone into shock based on her initial appearance. Her head injuries looked pretty scary as she had a severe gash in her front cranial. Blooding was spewing from somewhere and he wasn't certain of the extent. One of her legs was pinned underneath the steering wheel and her arm was contorted. He was a little dazed because he didn't expect it. She instantaneously retorted with "I am sorry, I just like to make the best out of odd situations"! She replied. He nodded, and gently touched her hand. He didn't look beyond her face very long he just wanted to provide comfort as she was probably more afraid than she was displaying verbally.

He and others scampered throughout the bus to assess the victims. Some were crying. Some were yelling. Some were frantic. Some were calm. Some were still unusually still.

Frank, another rescuer, moved over to the large lady who wasn't moving. He thought she was dead. A large piece of glass had fallen in on her lap. He thought it had punctured her internally but was uncertain. He immediately began praying aloud. She was still immobile. Others on the bus began to pray and stretch hands towards her direction as well. She slowly began to move. People all across the bus jeered in elation. The extent of the injuries weren't quite known yet but it appeared as if all would live.

By the next morning, the local newspaper, The City Venture, had the feature story of Jean Rogers, the bus driver, being a hero. They indicated it was her quick reaction to the bus being hit that possibly saved hundreds. It noted some of the known wounds to include Jean who had broken her pelvis and required surgery. She also endured a concussion which deemed 22 stitches, a broken arm, and a fractured tibia. Many passengers had experienced injuries from minor to severe fractures and broken bones. But the best news was that no one had died even after the numerous surgeries to print. It also highlighted the driver of the car which caused this tumultuous incident. She had broken her neck in two places; she severed her tibia and badly ruptured her clavicle bone. Her male passenger only had mere scrapes and bruises.

Ms. West, one of the most featured reporters had uncovered some details about the perpetrator's past. It was reported that she happened to have been the mistress of the local Interim Mayor who had just been secretly photographed with this same man who she was arguing with at the gas station. The former Mayor had died due to a severe heart attack and the Interim was still in his first 120 days after taking over this position. The picture had been released just 48 hours ago in another local publication.

Prior to the incident, she had probably not been revered as much as today. Despite being on her job for almost 4 years as an administrative assistant to a realtor, her world now was changing. She was discharged from work due to the unfavorable press she was receiving which definitely affected R&J Realty Firm. But her attitude and obvious disregard for those she had injured caused a heightened degree of disrespect for her. Within the article, it was learned that neither the police nor judge had any mercy on her. She alleged the bus and the other cars should have seen her coming although there were no signs of her applying the brakes prior to going into oncoming traffic. She even tried to name drop as she was friends with a few politicians. This just infuriated the detectives even more.

A messy situation with the Interim Mayor unfolded as he was on a conference trip with his assistants and team yet he was seen in a precarious situation with a significantly younger woman. It was rumored that while supposedly going down for his morning exercise in the hotel gym, he and this individual was seen chatting in a playful manner near the stairwell. His wife had been home and was planning their upcoming 10-year anniversary. She was actually 10 years his senior but they led a lifestyle which led most to believe it was utter happiness.

After communicating via phone for almost 8 or 9 months, Bob and Jean had formed quite a unique friendship. By the year anniversary of the accident, they had begun hanging out every once and a while. They would go out for coffee or meet for a movie. Sometimes they would just talk on the phone for hours.

As the years passed, their communication began to feel like they were destined to be family more so than just friends. Bob, now almost 35 and Jean, close to 65 were bosom buddies. They interestingly enough found the light-hearted side in most situations. When things were destined to be controversial they easily discussed their independent and mutual views as well.

Movie night was surreal as they shared quirky, odd laughs which only existed between the two. They mutually enjoyed reruns of *Carol Burnett, MASH, The Gong Show and Sanford & Sons.* Their favorite was *I Love Lucy and Mary Tyler Moore.* Every so often, they would even dance to the music from Soul Train. It was simply hilarious watching them do 'The Bump', 'The Twist', and especially 'The Robot'. Neither one could really dance but it was more about having fun than displaying rhythm. It was just pure, unadulterated enjoyment.

Surprisingly enough, during one of their hang out sessions, they both reminisced about their youth. Bob had rarely talked about his Mom, Annie, Stepdad or even Dad. But he was longing for the relationship with them that he never had. He grew up with various relatives over the year. Writing became second nature for him as this is how he learned to express himself. Jean never looked back as she had eventually revealed she came from an emotionally abusive home.

She wasn't angry but found solace in starting over even though she was all on her own. She heard the words, "it's better to be alone than with many feeling lonely".

Overall, Bob and Jean were a true duo. They laughed about the craziness they heard on the local radio stations. They laughed about the ridiculousness they observed from church. Like it or not; there was always subliminal drama if not about who was dating whom but if money was being allocated properly. Go figure!!! They laughed about the inconsistencies of politics. Neither of the two of them chose to openly discuss politics prior to their bond because more often than not; most people in work or friendly settings would take a simple conversation and cause it to become too out of control. They honestly found more similarities than not. They never engaged in crossing the delicate boundaries of friendship to relationship. It truthfully was not of interest to either of them.

Likewise, they closely followed the reports of then Interim Mayor and the tawdry female, Lydia, who had caused the terrible bus accident some time ago. According to recent tabloids, the younger woman had requested to meet with his wife. She apparently had some information to share with Pamela, who was still married to now Mayor Green. The meeting was quite interesting to say the least. It was revealed to Pamela by Lydia that she was actually was a ploy because she was helping the Mayor meet up with her brother who was a known activist for Gay rights. Truth be told, he wasn't just an activist. He was a well-known transgender who had been in a relationship with Mayor Green for some time. Mrs. Green was simply mortified as her life was spiraling out of control. She was truly astonished at the thought of her wonderful husband of a little over 10 years not only being accused of being a cheater but now being involved with a man. This was too much!!! As their relationship was trying to get back on track after all of this, to include rumors of divorce, they chose to try to move forward and heal as a family. But, this new development changed everything. As their 11th anniversary approached, Pamela chose not to simply rely on Mayor Green who continued to return home nightly and pretend as if all was well. The following Saturday after the two ladies met, Mrs. Green decided to take matters in her own hands. She was found dead in the presumed hotel room that her husband had been visiting on a regular basis. The suicidal note she wrote was ripped into pieces and placed next to her body, by her, as she felt she didn't need to justify the pain she had endured due to his selfishness. She took an overdose of Xanax and barbiturates. She just happened to have legal prescriptions due to her anxiety and other chronic pain illnesses. Mayor Green had questioned how she was granted entranced into room 311. It was simple for he truly thought this place was off limits to all except him and his antics. Pamela had been seen publicly for a while and was looked at as being regal and chic for her classy look stood out. Therefore, it was easy for her to get the hotel clerk to grant her entrance into the same room that her husband was rumored to have been in with 'his boy toy'. All she did was fabricated they were having a special night out together and requested this same room.

In the midst of all the public bitterness, Jean sat at home one day reflecting on how that terrible accident which was caused at the hands of a then suspected disgruntled mistress, Lydia, had actually been the result of a beautiful special relationship. It being the one she had now loved for many years with Bob. She glanced over and looked at the plant which was still growing nearby in the large tan flowerpot which he had given her some time ago when she was in the hospital. She never had a green thumb. But she truly thinks it grows because she talks to it, the plant, like it has human qualities. Subsequently, it grows and grows.

As she was sitting at her coffee table reminiscing over their friendship her mind took her back to an earlier encounter between the two. It was after her recovery period, in which the two of met for coffee at a local coffee shop which was notorious for relaxation and relaxed business meetings. It had such a special ambience. There were futons all throughout the shop which had retro style décor within. Its book racks were mounted on the walls and only required a finger imprint to check them out while in the shop drinking or snacking. The chic setting was second to none.

After a while, they began hanging out more and more. Jean still hadn't returned to work and had no immediate plans to do so. The combination of her residual side effects from the accident coupled with the upcoming trial was mentally exhausting to her. Her friend, Bob, always seemed to understand and find a way to make her laugh. He would occasionally call her and find the quirkiest things to talk about to minimize her stress. She so cherished their relationship.

One afternoon, Jean and Bob had a play date. They had ordered Italian food from the local Mama Rita, their favorite restaurant, which was notorious for being timely with delivery. Shortly after they ate, they went over to the sitting room and began chatting. Bob went into his room and returned with a large white envelope. Bob was excited to share with Jean his latest manuscript. He was working on a children's book. This was a little out of his normal genre as he customarily wrote science-fiction and mysteries. But this just felt right.

As he sat in the big brown chair and stared in anticipation, he was unquestionably nervous about her reaction to the new piece of work. He truly respected her opinion. He looked at her as she gave no facial indications. It was impossible to know if she was enjoying or was annoyed by what she was reading. He stared as she repositioned her body and shuffled in the comfortable tan oversized chair. He anxiously awaited her completion also he had some other news for her. Although Jean was a bus driver by trade now, she initially began as an English professor. She taught for almost 7 years then wanted a change. Her students and fellow colleagues were stunned but she never aspired to please others. She only wanted to ensure her students excelled in English. Therefore, some of her teaching methods were unorthodox but she had to do what felt right.

Another hour had passed then she glanced up with the most serious look. "Bob", she said in a very stern serious manner. He knew he was about to rip each and every page up because he dreaded the thought of it being totally horrific. "As you know, I greatly respect you and your brave courage for becoming an author after greatly searching for your passion and purpose. It takes so much to enter an industry which poses more questions than not. But, I truly don't understand." Jean just sat there and dropped her head. She knew he had won and lost many competitions for his writings.

She sat there without movement. She looked at the brother and confidant whom she had cherished for some time now. She was stunned and asked him where he was going for she saw him beginning to walk out of the room. "I am going to get the shredder. After listening to your true words of support, I know this piece of work obviously needs a restart". Bob was a little disappointed. But, he knew he was in this for the love and would only put out work that he should be proud of. "Man, chill," she said. "You precisely, phonetically, and profoundly engaged this audience in such a way that parents and children alike will be happy to become a part of your vast thinking!! I am utterly proud of you." The two of them affectionately hugged and the next hour went by rather quickly.

Before the two of them released their hug, she said, "I got it". He pushed her back and looked astoundingly at her. The only thing she said was "the kitten". She looked over on his bookshelf and saw two photos. One picture was of a brown kitten atop a shelf and the other with his sister lovingly holding the same kitten. The two of them smiled. Nothing else needed to be said.

Bob had almost forgotten that he had a wonderful proposition for her. "Jean, I want to introduce you to someone", he said. He went on to explain; this guy is 71, owns his own trucking business and has never been married. He is an avid traveler and . . ." She reached over and touched his lips. "Uh, no!!" she quickly uttered. "I like nothing old but money", she replied. I don't date old men not because they sometimes wear Depends and don't tell women. It's not because they are stubborn or stuck in their ways. But I have always thought younger than most. I enjoy the outrageous and exceptional way we communicate but I am not in the mood for an old man!!!" Jean laughed and laughed but was undeniably and sincerely honest about every word.

Bob tried on two more occasions over the next year or so to hook her up with his publisher and one other longtime friend. She was polite once and a little not so much so the second time. She went as far as to tell Bob that if he was really in the mood for hooking someone up, he could go on the date and enjoy the person for himself.

Shortly after that, he never tried again. Bob and Jean just did their friend 'thing' and they relished in that bond day in and day out. This was regardless if they talked daily or not!!!

Bob truly was blessed to have received a family—of one, Jean, after all these years. She was probably the only one to know the truth. His depression had slipped in over the last couple of days. It had overtaken his sleep and caused great sadness in the late hours of the evening. But to overcome he did his usual. He took out his stuffed kitten, which actually originally belonged to Annie, and cradled himself to sleep. His greatest secret was that he would cradle the stuffed animal or place the picture of his Mom and sister under his pillow to help him cope with his lifelong PTSD. In memory of them both, he places a small picture of a kitten on the last page of his manuscript. It's his way of ensuring they are with him to give him a personalized seal of approval.

ABOUT THE AUTHOR

Tracey 'Girlz' has been writing seriously since her high school days. She was privileged to have teachers who encouraged her creativity passion. They often fostered her desire to manipulate thoughts and ideas. To be honest, she was the secret writer of her high school newsletter. Early on, she wrote for B Visible Magazine, which is based in her hometown of Memphis, TN. Although she currently resides in South Carolina, she is more determined to forge forward in her lifelong endeavors. Her other marketing experiences include work in radio and television (formerly 'In the Midst with Tracey' host). Her educational accomplishments include a Certificate in Computerized Accounting, a BBA in Management from LeMoyne-Owen College and MSSW in Social Work from University of Tennessee. Her professional/social associations include Zeta Phi Beta Sorority, Inc., maintaining a relationship with her undergraduate alumni, and networking with other therapeutic professionals. Her 18 years of social service coupled with managerial and teaching experience has added to her base. Writing is simply a natural correlation of her innate desire to be a blessing to others. Prior to the term 'bucket list' becoming popular, she always knew she was destined to write a book. Although not currently teaching, she hopes to implore her ideal that (a) education is imperative; and (b) life is empirically shorter than we can conceive. Her two daughters, Dominique and Angel are a great part of who she is. Her hope is that others will realize they too can succeed and to not be held to the confines of others or a "box". To date, she enjoys being a mother, friend, sister, daughter, therapist, teacher, speaker, and writer. To be an author, is a lifelong dream and another accomplishment she is yet proud to add to her catalog of undertakings.